"I have hit upon a scheme," Lord Desmond explained.

"A scheme that will be beneficial to both of us. You see, I don't choose to be leg-shackled."

"Leg-shackled?" Samantha wrinkled her freckled nose.

"Married!" At her choke of amusement, he hurried on, "You don't know my mother. She's determined to attach me to some female before the season is out!"

Stunned with surprise, Sam listened while Mark unfolded his plan—how he would announce he was thinking of offering for her hand, so his mother would invite Sam and her sister to London for the season. The Scarborough sisters would avoid the prodigious expense of house, servants and chaperone, and Samantha's presence would protect Desmond from all other prospective brides.

"But why on earth would your mother feel induced to invite us?" Samantha asked bluntly.

"Because, Miss Scarborough, you are exactly what my mother has in mind for me—a young lady of the first respectability!"

D0804353

Dear Reader:

Welcome! We're glad you joined us for our new line, Harlequin Regency Romance. Two titles a month, every month, for your reading pleasure.

We know Regency readers want to be entertained, charmed and transported to that special time of magic and mischief. And we know you also like variety, so we've included everything from the Regency romp to the dramatic and touching love stories that Harlequin is famous for. We offer you authors you know and love, as well as new authors to discover and delight in. We feel we have captured the Regency spirit and are proud and pleased to share it with you.

Harlequin Regency Romance was created with you, the reader, in mind, and we'd like nothing better than to know what you think. If there's something special you would like to see included, drop us a line. If there's any way we can improve, we'd like you to tell us. We welcome your feedback and promise to consider it carefully. After all, you are our biggest fan.

We hope you enjoy reading Harlequin Regency Romance as much as we enjoyed putting it all together. And, in the true tradition of the Regency period, "we wish you happy" and look forward to hearing from you.

Marmie Charndoff
Editor

MATCHED PAIR

EVA RUTLAND

Harlequin Books

TORONTO • NEW YORK • LONDON
AMSTERDAM • PARIS • SYDNEY • HAMBURG
STOCKHOLM • ATHENS • TOKYO • MILAN

Dedicated to Jerlean Colley
for her help with "our book."

Published May 1989

ISBN 0-373-31101-X

CHAPTER ONE

THE TRAVELING COACH was well sprung and swayed easily, the joltings almost indiscernible even when they turned off the main highway onto the rough country roads. The young man inside the coach lounged against the soft cushions, smiling to himself.

He had won the bet fair and square, and was now on his way to take his pick of the Scarborough Stables. Probably he would choose Black Knight, the stallion that had taken the third heat at Newmarket, outdistancing his own Silver Grey by a length. That had cost him several guineas, too.

"Well, you are mine now, you beautiful beast," he muttered in satisfaction. But maybe not. The Scarborough Stables were noted throughout several counties for their horse flesh and he meant to pick the very best.

He chuckled, remembering the look on Stanley Scarborough's face when the winning dice went down. But he had just thrown up his hands in good humour.

"Damme, Desmond! Your luck has to run out sometime. All right. Meet me at Scarborough on the tenth and take your pick. Ain't we due at Rutherford's on the twelfth? My place is on the way. I can go on with you."

You couldn't say Scarborough was a poor loser. Good thing, since he lost more often than he won. Lord Desmond leaned back comfortably, anticipating the pleasures ahead. He'd send Black Knight back with his groom and go on to Lord Rutherford's for a week of hunting. He'd be back in London in time for Angel's opening night. In time, he hoped, to pick up some trinket in honour of the occasion. Something that would make her eyes sparkle and her voluptuous lips make promises of proper thanks.

Then two weeks later the London season would begin, and he had promised his mother... Oh, Lord, why had he promised her? His mother had caught him in a weak moment. Bound to be a weak moment, breakfasting before ten!

He had come into her small breakfast parlour stifling a yawn. There she was, as fresh as the morning dew, her blond hair with its almost imperceptible strands of grey piled high on her head. She refused to wear a cap, and he didn't blame her. She still retained her youthful figure, and, in her frilly pink dressing gown, looked as pretty and delicate as the roses on the table.

Delicate she was not. "Darling," she greeted him as he bent over to kiss her, "I hated to have Atwood rouse you so early, but I wanted to talk with you before you left. Quite seriously. Get your breakfast, then come and sit with me."

Desmond lifted the silver cover of the chafing dish and served himself two baked eggs, then added a slice of ham and some kippers.

She poured him a cup of coffee and began a long discourse on the importance of his settling down and quitting his ramshackle ways.

"Ramshackle? Mama!"

"Well, I don't precisely mean that. But, Mark, dear, you do run about so. Now when your father was ill—"

"But he's quite recovered now."

"Yes, yes, I know, and I'm very thankful for that. But while he was ill, you did settle down, and I must say you took very good care of affairs here. Even Jenson says his grace would not have done better himself."

"Quite gallant of him, considering all I did was say, 'Do you think so, Jenson? Very well, Jenson, do what you think best.'"

She threw up her hands. "You are abominable! I'm sure Jenson is a very good steward, but he has no authority and could do nothing without your direction, which I am persuaded was excellent. He certainly gives all credit to you."

"Perhaps I should have Father increase his wages."

"That indeed might be a very good thing. So trustworthy. I can always depend upon him even if your father is ill and you are off to the races or the gaming houses or wherever you go with your petticoat girls."

His lips twitched. "The term is 'light skirts,' Mother."

"Exactly. The thing is, Mark, if you could just be seen in the proper places. If you'd just spend one season in London."

"Oh, Mother, not Almack's. Not again. I did it once and you almost had me leg shackled to the most insipid creature."

"Insipid! Pamela Moorhead? Why, she's the most gorgeous—"

"A dead bore."

"How can you say such a thing? So mannerly. And that hair, as black as yours, and that ivory skin. Such a handsome couple you made. I'm sure they would have been beautiful!"

He was buttering another scone, but looked up at this. "They?"

"Your children, dear."

He shook his head in exasperation, but could only mutter, "Nonsense!"

"There is certainly nothing nonsensical about it! You are a remarkably handsome man. Tall, like your father, with the same broad shoulders and the same dark eyes. With your eyes and her hair and her...no, not her mouth. Much too thin, don't you think?"

He laughed. "I think Pamela's children will have her mouth and her earl's bulging eyes, and I'm thankful for that. If he had not offered for her I'm sure you and Aunt Julia would have had me in his place—with all those carefully arranged tête-à-têtes."

"Now that's a ridiculous notion. You know very well we could not have offered for you."

"A very providential circumstance."

"Oh, you needn't be sarcastic. Indeed, it might be a very good thing if we could offer for you. We'd never let you get mixed up with those muslin skirts."

Desmond laughed, almost choking on his coffee. "Mixed up, I might be. But never married, Mama."

His mother sniffed. "Some of those creatures can be quite beguiling, I believe. And you never know. Men can be so gullible." She turned a serious face toward him. "Remember Lord Atterley? I'm sure he never meant to be married to that shockingly common Lenora Lindsey, and you know what came of that. You have to think of your position, Mark."

"Shall I bring the lady for your inspection before I offer?" he asked playfully.

"No, you needn't promise anything like that, for I know you never would. But, Mark, darling, do think of your position. You are a marquis."

He sighed. "Yes, I know."

"And don't shake your head like that. You may as well face up to it. You are the sole heir to Somerset and a considerable fortune."

"I know, I know."

"And the truth is," his mother continued, "you will never find a proper wife among the linen markets."

"Muslin company."

"Precisely. The thing is, you must be in the proper places, attend the proper assemblies to meet a lady."

"Oh, no, Mother. Not Almack's. I'll not stand around and pay court to—to all those simpering, purring, cajoling females."

"Do you mean to tell me your lights o' love don't purr and cajole?"

"Well, they ain't angling for a wedding ring," he said, thinking she was right about the cajoling. Angel had been hinting for several weeks now for a high-perched phaeton and a matched pair.

The duchess touched his hand. "Mark, you have to think of your father."

"Father?" He looked at her anxiously.

"Oh, he's all right now, except that his gout is acting up. But he does worry so—about the succession. He was late marrying himself and considers himself lucky that his only child was a son. You are already thirty-two and not yet married."

She had gone on then about his father's concerns, but Mark did not set much store in this. He knew the problem was his mother's desire for grandchildren and her fear that he might become seriously entangled with someone completely unacceptable. But his mother also had a cajoling way about her, and before he knew it, he had promised to be in attendance during the London season. It would not much signify. Angel was never available until after theatre hours and the gaming halls were open all night.

His mother thanked him profusely, declaring that he might be surprised at all the new faces. Dear Lady Campbell's darling Kate, for instance, was to make her come out this season.

This was when he became apprehensive. Lady Campbell was his mother's dearest friend, and, if his memory was correct, her darling Kate was a little too plump, with buck teeth. Oh, well, he thought, the season was a month away.

The discussion with his mother had delayed him, and he had had to put up last night at a wayside inn. No matter. The morning air was refreshing and he'd be at Scarborough long before noon. He tilted his hat over his face, leaned back and, lulled by the swaying chaise, was soon asleep.

He was jerked awake and jolted out of his seat when the chaise came to an abrupt halt. As he sought to regain his hat and his composure, he heard a feminine voice crying out in great agitation. But the voice was drowned out by the shouts of Jiggs, his coachman.

"What in thunderation are you about, you silly minx! You almost got trampled, grabbing the bridle like that!"

Emerging from the coach, Lord Desmond found that the coachman was addressing a young girl who was still clinging desperately to the lead horse's bridle.

"Help me, please! I didn't mean to upset you."

"Upset me?" The coachman mopped his brow. "Plague take it, you scared the living daylights out of me. Had to pull strong to the left. What the devil are you about?"

"I had to stop you. Oh, be still, you vexatious beast. Oh, no, not you, sir. I fear I have frightened your horses."

Desmond watched in some amusement as the girl, obviously more concerned for the horse than for his driver, sought to soothe the frightened animal. The horse became calm.

The driver did not. "To come flying out like that! And on a quiet country road where one ain't expecting it like one would in the middle of London—"

"Oh, will you stop your silly prattle and listen!" The girl stamped her foot and her voice had an authoritative ring.

Damned impertinent for a country wench! And that's surely what she was, thought Desmond, despite that high-toned accent. Now how did that come about, he puzzled, surveying the faded muslin gown and the stout country shoes. She did not even have the genteel appearance of a ladies' maid.

But she was a beauty! She was bareheaded and her hair was a mass of tangled bronze curls. Or were they red? She had an elfin face and there was a sprinkle of freckles across the small nose. She seemed immediately to regret her impertinence and now lifted a pair of apologetic but incredibly large green eyes to the coachman.

"Pray, don't be angry with me. I do so need your help."

Ah, thought Desmond, a pretty damsel in distress. His stay at Scarborough could be quite diverting. He moved forward and extended his hand. "How may we be of service to you, ma'am?"

Apparently noticing Desmond for the first time, the girl relaxed her hold on the bridle and turned those troubled green eyes to him. "It's Haro. Oh, please sir. Please hurry." Without ceremony she grabbed his outstretched hand and pulled him toward the forest.

Desmond glanced back at Clinton, his groom, seated beside Jiggs. Clinton, who had been enjoying the spectacle immensely, jumped down and followed.

The girl gasped as she ran. "He's caught in some horrible trap and I can't release the spring. Oh, please hurry."

Haro was a beautiful spaniel, and he was indeed caught in one of those despicable traps. Desmond felt a surge of hot anger, almost feeling the pain himself as he watched the trapped animal struggle to release himself. The dog growled as they approached, but when Desmond bent and stroked the silky head, the growl became a pleading whine.

"Now, now, lie still. Patience, old fellow. We'll soon have you out of here." Desmond examined the trap carefully. It was crudely made, just needing force to release it. The dog gave a yelp of pain and struggled to rise as his leg was freed. Desmond pushed him gently back. "Not yet. Lie still. There. Now let's see about this leg."

The girl helped, cradling the dog's head in her lap, while Desmond felt the injured leg. Thank God, it was not mangled.

"It's broken, but a clean break," he said to the anxious girl. His eyes searched the ground for some sort of support. Anticipating his need, Clinton produced a sturdy stick.

"Now I need something with which to bind it," Desmond muttered.

Without hesitation, the girl lifted her skirt. He caught sight of a slender and enticingly shaped ankle above the rough shoe. Showing no concern for propriety or his appreciative eyes, she hurriedly tore a strip from her petticoat and handed it to him.

Ah, he thought as he bound the dog's leg, *the delicious freedom of country wenches.*

"There. That should hold it." He gave the dog a gentle pat, then turned to the girl. "He should stay off that leg for a while."

"Yes, I'll see that he does. Oh, sir, you have been so kind. It was providential that you were passing."

She went on to thank him quite prettily, but Desmond hardly attended. He had taken care of the dog, reassured himself that the creature was not maimed, and could now centre his interest on the dog's pretty mistress. He watched with fascination the dimple that disappeared and reappeared at the corner of her mouth as she talked.

She said she hated to impose on him further, but, as he was going in that direction, would he have his coachman stop and convey a message?

Here the marquis interrupted. There was something quite beguiling about this tousled miss, and he meant to improve on the acquaintance.

"You're not imposing," he said. "And there's no need for a message. We will be glad to convey you and your dog to your destination. Clinton, bring a blanket."

When they were settled in the coach, the dog on a blanket between them, the marquis attempted to better the acquaintance. He began with the obvious. "Do you live near here?"

"Just a mile up the road. We won't take you out of your way, will we, Haro? There now, my pet. We'll soon have something to ease the pain." She concentrated on the dog and did not look at Desmond.

The marquis was not accustomed to women who did not look at him. He was no macaroni and was often the despair of his valet. But women were always commenting on his powerful build and his handsome face. Nor did they fail to notice the shine on his Hessians or the cut of his weskit. Now this strange chit seemed unaware of his many virtues, nor did she seem impressed by the chaise built and furnished in the latest style. And, he reflected ruefully, she did not seem concerned about the cakes of dirt she and her dog were distributing about its luxurious interior.

Still, she was an entrancing hoyden. Small, almost childlike. But there was nothing childlike about the contours of the rounded bosom—provocative even in that ill-fitting muslin gown. And any girl who turned her back on him and stared out a window was a challenge to Lord Desmond. Well, flattery always worked. "Amazing," he said in his most admiring tones. "The colour of autumn leaves!"

She did not ask the obvious question; indeed, she seemed not to hear him.

"Your hair," he said, feeling a little stupid. "It's quite beautiful."

"I wonder," she said, this time staring out the opposite window, affording him an excellent view of her other profile.

"No doubt about it," he assured her, imagining that tangled mass of curls spread upon a straw mattress in some Scarborough hayloft. "It's such a striking colour."

"I wonder who could have set it."

"What?" He was puzzled.

"That trap. It's bad enough when a band of people chase one lone fox with a pack of hungry dogs."

He stirred restlessly. Could she know that he was on his way to a fox hunt?

"But to set a trap," she continued, "where a poor little animal could be crippled and left to die slowly. Oh, it's too cruel. I wonder if it could have been the Benton boy."

Not knowing the Benton boy, he could only shrug.

"Well, it shan't happen again, I promise you, Haro." She spoke in soothing tones, one hand lightly petting the dog.

Desmond took the hand in his own and smiled at her. "Perhaps, since we are travelling together, we should introduce ourselves. My name is Desmond."

"*Lord* Desmond?"

She did look at him then and there was utter contempt in her deep green eyes. The look was veiled as the long lashes went quickly downward. But he had seen it all right, and he didn't understand it. What the devil did the girl have against him? She didn't even know him.

"Your name?" he prompted.

"Samantha Scarborough."

"Scarborough!" he stuttered. Oh, yes, he had heard that Stanley Scarborough had inherited a couple of nieces along with the property. But what was Scarborough's niece doing running around the country like some country wench? And acting like one—the way she'd grabbed that bridle and stopped his horses.

"A relation of Lord Stanley Scarborough?" he asked.

"His niece."

Well—damme! There ended the flirtation that had never begun. He didn't trifle with ladies of quality, and Miss Scarborough was a lady, even if she didn't act like one.

"Oh, well, it's a pleasure to meet you, Miss Scarborough," he said, remembering his manners. "And you certainly are not taking me out of the way. I'm to meet your uncle at Scarborough."

She seemed to be struggling for composure herself. "It was indeed wonderful that you came along when you did. I am so grateful."

She was all politeness. But there was that—that— Why the devil didn't she like him? What had he ever done to her? No matter! Idiotic little wretch. Nothing on her mind but traps and dogs.

CHAPTER TWO

STARING OUT THE WINDOW, Samantha Scarborough had a good deal on her mind besides traps and dogs. So this was Mark Desmond! How many times she had heard that hateful name! How many times had Uncle Stanley come seeking Papa's aid!

"So you are in the suds to Mark Desmond again," Papa would shout. "That deep! Good God, Stanley! If you must keep gaming, why don't you keep to your limit?"

When his brother prattled about gentlemen and debts of honour, her father gave a stinging retort. "It ain't honour I'm talking about, Stanley. It's pockets. Desmond's are pretty plump and yours are out to let."

Stanley would laugh at that, declare that nothing risked meant nothing gained, and then he'd recall a big stake he had won some months before.

Her father threw up his hands. "There seems to be some laxity in reporting your gains. It only comes to my notice when you take a fall. Which is why I believe it incumbent upon you to steer clear of Mark Desmond. He's well padded and can sustain a loss! You can't!"

Papa would berate him, but he usually gave Uncle Stanley whatever he asked. In spite of Kemper.

Mrs. Kemper was not one to hold her tongue. She had come to the house as a parlour maid when the Scarborough boys were young, and now, as their housekeeper, she considered herself their guardian.

"So Master Stanley's here to pull on your purse strings again," she declared to Lord Scarborough.

George Scarborough had only laughed. "Well, yes. It's the company he keeps. The Desmond crowd. More plump in the pocket than he."

Mrs. Kemper regarded him with keen eyes. "You ain't got no cause to feel guilty, Lord Mr. George, because you're the elder son and got the property. That's the way it's always been and that's as it should be. Besides, he had his own independence. His old lordship saw to that. And it ain't your fault Mr. Stanley gambled it all away."

"I fear he is a bit of a gamester. Pity."

Mrs. Kemper sniffed. "A pity since he's always gaming that he ain't winning sometimes. And a pity you ain't learned that giving money to Mr. Stanley is like pouring it through a sieve."

Remembering this conversation, Samantha saw that it should have been a warning. Even so, what could she have done? They had been so grief stricken, she and her sister, Emily, by the untimely death of their father, over a year ago now. They had welcomed the kindhearted uncle who had grieved with them, who had questioned the wisdom of an Almighty who had not had the foresight to take him in the place of the steady, reliable George.

"George was the rock," he explained to the girls. "I am the rolling stone." Then, seeing the frightened look on their faces, he sought to comfort them in his own awkward way. "There, there, don't take on so." He smoothed Emily's curls and seemed not to notice the mess she was making of his impeccable neckcloth.

Then he looked at Samantha, sitting stiff and silent on the sofa, and gave her just the opposite advice. "Let it out, girl, let it out. Breaks your heart to hold it in. Have yourself a good cry." He looked so helpless with one girl crying on his shoulder, the other so still and quiet. "Brandy," he said, "that's the ticket." He rang the bell for Kemper. "We need a bracer. Bring a bottle of brandy, Mrs. Kemper."

Then, taking note of Kemper's squelching look, he stammered. "No—no, not the thing. Tea. That's the ticket. A spot of good tea." He looked again at the girls, then called to Kemper, who was on her way out. "Bring a little brandy for me. Just for me, you understand."

Fortified by the brandy, he prepared to assume his responsibilities, assuring them that things would go on as always. He would be as good a father as he could. "I ain't much in the petticoat line. Well, that is, in a family way," he amended. "But you know I love you and I'll try to do my best for you."

Well, thought Samantha, *that* he had tried to do. To the detriment of them all. For Uncle Stanley seemed unable to deny anyone, including himself, anything they wanted.

How was it Simmons, the bailiff, had put it last week when he felt compelled to appeal to Samantha? "You have to speak to him, Miss Samantha. Somebody has to. He's scandalously reckless in his spending and heedless of his obligations."

Samantha stared at him, speechless, and he mopped his brow and went on. "Now that he's inherited the property, there's no one to cry halt. He takes no interest in the running of the estate and we are in pretty desperate straits."

"But, Simmons, I thought . . . That is, you have always managed so well."

"The truth is, miss, that when he came into the money, he sent all these bills from London and I had to dig into the capital. And every time we make a bit of profit, he presents us with these staggering debts." The harassed little man nervously polished his spectacles with his handkerchief. "Now we are having to sell off some of the stallions, and Hawkins is beside himself. You see, that means the stud fees are sharply reduced."

"Oh, no," Samantha cried, quite overcome at the thought of losing the horses so carefully bred by her father. "You can't do that, Simmons. You can use some of my money. I—"

"No, Miss Samantha. Mr. Stanley says I am on no account to touch yours or Miss Emily's inheritance. And, even if he were willing, I'd advise against it. We are indeed fortunate that the property is entailed and cannot be mortgaged."

"Things are that bad?"

He nodded. "And getting worse. If you could just speak to him and try to get him to hold off on his spending. I'd hate to sell off more stock. The thing is, it's two months before the quarterly rents are due. And the Joneses' cottage needs a new roof. Well, you see how it is, miss." He mopped his brow again. "If somebody don't stop him, he'll end up in the sponging house and we'll be in utter ruin."

Samantha had promised to talk to Lord Scarborough, but since he was in London she had had no opportunity. He'd arrived late last night, and she would do it today. But now, here was this guest, Lord Desmond! Good heavens! She gave the gentleman beside her a sharp glance. Was it possible that he had come to collect a bet?

The chaise had turned into the courtyard now, and Lord Scarborough came out to greet his guest. "Well, Desmond, my boy. You're in damme good time. Nuncheon in an hour. I'll have Mrs. Kemper set another place. Samantha? You there? What's amiss?"

Lord Desmond explained, and Stanley moved to examine the dog. "There, there, lie still, old fellow. Wait till they get you to Hawkins. He'll fix you up all right and tight. Devilish bad thing, traps! But where? We don't allow traps about the place, do we, Sam?"

Samantha said they did not and he should have Simmons discover who set it.

"Haro don't look too bad," Lord Scarborough declared. "Don't worry, Sam. Hawkins knows what to do." Bidding a lackey to fetch Lord Desmond's bag and directing the coachman to the stable, he led his guest into the house, his mind on quite another subject. "Did you get to the Hungerford mill? Did Cribbs win?"

"He did not," said Desmond. "Belcher left him pretty well banged up."

"Damnation! I laid a monkey Cribbs would win. Had two hundred guineas on him, the big bruiser."

An anxious look on her face, Samantha watched them disappear into the house. But she remained in the coach, one hand restraining Haro. Only to Hawkins would she release him.

Hawkins, the head groom and horse trainer, an expert with broken bones and torn ligaments, declared that his lordship had done a first-rate job in setting the leg.

"He was extremely careful," Samantha said, remembering how gentle he had been and how unquestioningly he had come to her aid. She would not have expected it of Lord Desmond. Giving Haro a final pat, she left him to the ministrations of Hawkins and returned to the house, where she was roundly scolded by Mrs. Kemper.

"Looking so frowsy when there's a guest in the house. It ain't seemly, Miss Samantha. Miss Emily says you're to drive her to Pendleton, where you're both expected for nuncheon. Just as well, since no one informed me we were to have a guest and we've only a beef roast and yorkshire pudding. I told Cook to add a brace of pigeons and parsnips. Still, that doesn't seem quite the meal for a marquis."

Samantha said to tell Cook to add some of her famous apple tarts and that would be just fine. Upstairs, she dressed quickly and then went to fetch Emily.

With the help of Jenny, the upstairs maid, Emily was engrossed in arranging her blond curls in the style of a picture spread before them. She gave one satisfied glance at her reflection and turned to Samantha. "Oh, Sam, I'm glad you didn't forget that you're driving me over to Pendleton. Arthur's starting my portrait this morning. Do you like this hairstyle?"

"Very pretty."

"Arthur says I have perfect classic features and this picture was in *Modes and Manners*—the perfect coiffure for the lady of elegance. Jenny copied it. See?"

Samantha compared the picture with the finished product. "An excellent likeness. You are very clever, Jenny."

"Thank you, miss."

"Yes, you are clever," said Emily. "I may take you to London with me. You could be my dresser."

Jenny's eyes lighted at the prospect, but when Samantha suggested that Mrs. Kemper might need her, she hurried away.

Emily slipped into a beige walking dress modishly bound in silk braid. "Wasn't it fortunate that Uncle brought this dress for me? It's just the thing for my portrait and so elegant. It's all the crack in London."

"Emily," Samantha said as she began to button her sister's dress. "I don't want you to ask Uncle Stanley to take you to London."

"Not ask him!"

"Do be still, Emily. I haven't finished."

"But, Samantha, he's so scatterbrained. He'd never think of it himself."

"Exactly." Samantha fastened the last button and stepped back.

Emily faced her, eyes smouldering. "Samantha, you are horribly mean and selfish. You don't want me to go to London."

"It's just not the time."

"It certainly is the time. I should have gone last year, only Papa died, and of course I would not wish to go then.

But now I'm a whole year older. You want me to be an old spinster like yourself."

"No, Emily. Please listen."

"I will not listen. You are two and twenty and not married. I should think you would want to go."

"Well, yes, I would, but—"

"No, you wouldn't. You don't care a fig about balls. You'd rather be stuck in a stable. But I will have a come out. Oh, bother, where's that shoe? You had your come out."

"That was different." Samantha retrieved the shoe from under the dresser and handed it to her. "Aunt Agatha was living then."

"And what has that to do with anything?"

"Uncle would have to hire a house and staff it and Simmons says—"

"Simmons! That stingy old bailiff. What has he to say to anything?" Emily searched in her drawer for a handkerchief. "Uncle makes the decisions and he never says no to anything."

Nothing was more true than that. "Emily, he can't afford it."

"And it's not your decision, either! You had your chance. You went to London for your come out."

"I hated it." Samantha thought of standing up at Almack's, conscious only of her funny-coloured hair and the freckles that were never quite erased by Aunt Agatha's lemon-and-cucumber lotion.

"Well, I would not hate it."

That was true. Emily would love it. Emily with the full figure and the corn-coloured curls, the big blue eyes and the porcelain complexion, never marred by wind or sun.

Was she jealous of Emily? No, Samantha thought. Emily should have her chance and she would be perfectly willing to accompany her. She was reconciled to suffering all the tortures of another London season just for Emily's sake. But Simmons had made such dire predictions. "Emily," she confided, "Simmons told me that Uncle is in a very poor way, even hovering on the brink of debtor's prison."

Emily stared at her. "That's not true. How could he be poor? All this property is his. And look at all the fine clothes he wears. And his carriages. And all the gifts he brings. He couldn't do that if he were poor." Emily was not convinced of Uncle Stanley's difficulties. It was Samantha who blocked her way. "It's not fair. Just because you didn't catch a husband doesn't mean someone won't offer for me."

Samantha thought of the earl with the spindly legs and foul breath who had offered for her. Aunt Agatha had said he was rich and she was not to be a goose. She had been glad to be called home in the middle of the season. Sorry Papa was ill, but glad that he had needed her, and glad to escape.

"Emily," she said slowly, "you don't need to go to London to catch a husband. Indeed, I thought you were rather fond of Arthur."

"Arthur Travis? That child!"

"He's two years older than you. And not too young, I perceive, to paint your portrait."

"Well, he is an artist, and he said I had a perfect profile. Oh, Sam, I am fond of him, but he's excessively lacking in . . . in dash! And he's just a plain mister!"

"Oh, you have some particular title in mind?"

"At Almack's you meet all the ton. And Jenny says I'm just the type to make a fine duchess."

"Oh," Samantha said again. "And how many duchesses does Jenny number among her acquaintances?"

"You are abominable! You don't have to know a duchess to know how one should look. I will go to Almack's. And you needn't. You can just stay here and marry one of your stupid horses!" Tears welled up in the deep blue eyes.

"Oh, Emily, if you're going to have a fit of the vapours, those perfect features will be too swollen for Arthur to put on canvas."

This logical observation brought an abrupt end to the tears. Emily dabbed at her eyes, took one anxious look in the mirror and stormed out.

On the drive to Pendleton, Emily was sulkily silent. But as soon as they were settled in Lady Travis's small informal dining room, she talked incessantly, complaining of the come out due her and how excessively selfish some people were.

Samantha frowned. It was true that Lady Travis was a dear friend and had been like a mother to them since their own mother had died ten years earlier. But some things should not be discussed outside the family. She was glad when Arthur's appearance interrupted the discussion.

A tall blond young man, Arthur was attired in a smock and beret of the type affected by artists. Samantha stifled a giggle. It was unkind of Emily to say that Arthur was lacking in dash when he tried so hard. Last year he had swaggered around in skintight boots, pantaloons and sash in pugilistic style. The year before that, in a beaver and a coat with an abundance of capes, he had driven his gig over the country roads with breakneck speed.

"Arthur," Emily cried, "I wondered where you were."

"I was getting things set up." He scratched his nose and took a critical look at Emily. "Good Lord, Emily, why did you wear that dress? I told you to wear the blue!"

"Arthur," her ladyship murmured, "surely you are not going to dine in that . . . that costume."

"Oh, Mama, I am not going to dine at all. Hello, Samantha. Emily, are you finished? I want to catch the sun."

Samantha smiled a greeting and his mother pressed him to stay for tea and cakes.

"No, thank you, Mama. Come on, Emily. Why the devil did you wear that dress?"

"It's the latest fashion," Emily protested.

"Fashion!" he exclaimed as the two departed. "What I want is colour."

"I suppose," said Lady Travis, looking after them, "that it is a good hobby, but it is rather impractical."

"It is indeed fortunate," Samantha interposed, "that it is not a matter of money and Arthur can indulge any hobby he chooses."

"Nevertheless it would please Sir John if he took more interest in the estate. Some hobbies are more in keeping with his station. Take your father for instance—what he did with his interest in horses."

"A very good thing he had that interest," said Samantha, "for it was a question of money and he certainly brought Scarborough out of the suds. It's a good thing he was a baron, too," she added with a laugh, "or else he would have been dubbed a common horse trader."

"Nevertheless he was a baron, and there are certain things due to the daughters of a baron," Lady Travis scolded. "You do see the force of Emily's logic, don't you? Of course, I had thought that Emily and Arthur would...but that's beside the point. A lady likes the chance to look around before she settles down. Sir John is even thinking of sending Arthur up for a little town polish."

Samantha said nothing.

Lady Travis picked up a cup and set it down. She looked at Samantha and her voice took on an inquiring, almost apologetic tone. "I have seen Sir Thomas, the squire, riding toward your place rather often lately."

"Oh, Lady Travis, not you, too. Please, make no conjectures about myself and the squire."

"Well, Samantha, your absence was rather conspicuous at his assembly last night. But, my dear, if you have no interest in that quarter, it would be the best of all things for you to go to London."

Samantha stiffened. "Why is it that everyone supposes a lady must always be on the lookout for a husband?"

"My dear girl, it is the most natural thing in the world. Whatever else are you to do? And for ladies of quality like ourselves, why, not to go to London for the season is unthinkable. I wonder your uncle has not proposed it himself."

"He—he's been busy," Samantha stammered.

"Of course, he should have to find a sponsor for you. But that should not signify. He is in and out of London all the time and must number among his acquaintances." Here Lady Travis paused, staring fixedly at one of the raisin cakes. "But Sir John says he spends a good deal of time with Lord Desmond's crowd...." Her voice trailed off in embarrassed confusion.

There was that name again. Lord Desmond. Lord Desmond set a wicked pace.

"Well," said Lady Travis, "I am sure he could get a sponsor for you. Someone who could procure vouchers at Almack's."

Samantha jumped up. "I forgot. I promised Mrs. Kemper I would return early. An errand...a guest. I'd better go." She couldn't discuss it. Talking about Uncle Stanley was like biting the hand that fed her.

The good lady promised to have Arthur convey Emily home, and advised Samantha to take heed of what she had said. Of all things a season in London would be best.

"Yes," agreed Samantha, escaping as soon as she could.

The groom brought her curricle around and helped Samantha up. Her gloved hand gave the reins an expert flick, setting Bonnie off at a brisk trot. Samantha loved the high-stepping Bonnie, her favourite bay mare. She loved the shiny new curricle, one of Uncle's latest gifts. So many gifts! So generous! So foolish.

CHAPTER THREE

SHE HAD NOT had time to speak with Uncle Stanley. Mrs. Kemper advised her to dress for dinner, suggesting she not wear the old grey frock but one of the new ones her uncle had brought from London.

Upstairs in her room, Samantha washed and carefully brushed her hair. Then she selected a brown dress with a fresh white lace collar. She rejected any of the gowns her uncle had brought, for she thought bright colours clashed with her hair.

Downstairs, the drawing room looked cosy and festive, with the lit candles glowing against polished oak and a fire burning on the hearth.

Both Lord Scarborough and his guest were dressed for dinner. Lord Scarborough, impeccable as always, was dressed in buff coloured breeches and a yellow velvet coat. Lord Desmond's dark hair was tied neatly back with a narrow black riband. He wore a blue coat and flowered weskit.

Emily had changed into a blue silk dress which exactly matched her eyes and was talking animatedly to Lord Desmond, who was smiling down at her. Arthur Travis, whom Emily had invited for dinner before she knew of the new, fascinating guest, was sitting disconsolately on the sofa.

"And this," said Lord Scarborough, "is my other niece. Oh, I forgot. You've already met Sam, haven't you?"

"Well, I thought I had. But now I am not so sure." Lord Desmond moved toward her, a mischievous and rather disconcerting twinkle in his dark eyes. "This proper lady in no way resembles the waif I met on the road this afternoon."

Oh, dear, Samantha thought, *I must have looked a fright.* But she gazed frankly up at him. "Well, sir, I know you. You are the kind gentleman who came to my rescue when I was quite distressed. I hope I remembered to thank you properly."

"Oh, you did." He seemed to be quietly studying her, and she felt a flush rise to her cheeks.

"Samantha," Emily broke in, "did you know that Lord Desmond drove his curricle from London to Brighton in less than four hours? What do you think of that?"

"I think it must have been very hard on his poor horses," Samantha answered.

"And pretty hard on my purse." Lord Scarborough paused in the act of taking snuff from an elegant gold snuff box. "I bet five hundred pounds he couldn't do it under four hours."

"Oh, you were so brave," Emily said to the marquis. "I would have been scared to death. Weren't you afraid your curricle would overturn?"

"No, it was specially made," Desmond replied, but he was looking at Samantha. "You don't approve, I take it?"

"It does seem rather hard, my lord, to spring your horses at such a wicked pace for four hours."

"Three hours and fifty-six minutes." Stanley groaned. "Just four minutes between me and a thousand pounds."

"I thought you said five hundred, Lord Scarborough." Arthur was aghast at the thought of such high stakes.

"Well, that'd be five hundred I would have won, and five hundred I wouldn't have to pay out. Make it a thousand, don't it?"

"You don't approve of racing, Miss Scarborough?" Lord Desmond asked.

"Oh yes, she does." Anxious to bring his lordship's attention back to herself, Emily answered for Samantha. "Samantha'd rather go to Newmarket than to a ball, so I don't see why she's making such a fuss over your racing your curricle to Brighton."

Desmond's eyebrows went up. "Newmarket? You attend the races there?"

Samantha felt her cheeks go hot. He probably thought, as Mrs. Kemper did, that it was not proper for a lady to do so. "Not since my father died, sir." She did not think it necessary to add that without Mrs. Kemper's approval, Hawkins would not take her.

"Well, well, I think they do spring their horses there."

"Not for four hours, my lord, and not on a crowded highway." She answered firmly and turned to seat herself beside Arthur.

"Sam's devilish precise about such things," Lord Scarborough pointed out. "Matter of fact, she's devilish precise about anything concerning a horse."

Lord Desmond seemed about to pursue the subject, but was restrained by Emily, who declared she was tired of talking about horses and races. "Now me, I just love a ball. Do you like to dance, Lord Desmond? Are you often at Almack's?"

Feeling a pang of sympathy for the rejected Arthur, Samantha made an effort to engage him. "How is the painting going?"

Arthur was not to be diverted. Torn between jealousy of Emily and adulation of the man he considered a Corinthian, he could not look away from the engaging pair. "That dress," he complained, "that's what she should have worn this morning."

When Samantha explained it was hardly a morning frock, he said what did that have to do with anything, when she was sitting for her portrait and he had particularly asked that she wear colour.

Samantha was glad when Porter announced dinner.

Emily slipped her arm through Desmond's, saying they should go in together as they were such a good match. "My blue dress and your blue coat, you know."

Arthur's frown was not erased, though Samantha declared she was the lucky one to have two escorts—the handsomest man in the room and her favourite uncle.

Mrs. Kemper had enlarged upon Samantha's suggested menu and Cook had prepared a meal suitable for noble company. After soup was removed, Porter brought in a brace of pigeons and a leg of lamb with spinach, as well as the roast beef and Yorkshire pudding.

During dinner, Emily managed rather cleverly to keep the conversation on London. She plied Lord Desmond and her uncle with questions about the museum, the waxworks, Covent Gardens. By the time the sweetmeats were served, she evoked the question she had been angling for all evening.

"But have you never been to London, my dear?"

"Not I. Samantha has." Ignoring Samantha's frown, Emily went on. "Her come out, you know when she was seventeen. Of course, when I was seventeen Papa had died, and there was the mourning period and it would not have been proper, and of course I should not have wanted to go then." She finished on a plaintive note. "I have never been and I should so much like to go."

Desmond gave his host a disapproving look. "How unkind of you, Scarborough, to keep two such beauties hidden in the country!"

But the reproof was unnecessary. Lord Scarborough clapped his hand to his forehead and uttered a cry of dismay. "By Jove! What a jackanapes I've been!" He pointed his dessert fork at Emily and exclaimed, "London! Of course you want to go, and you shall go!"

"Oh, Uncle, do you mean it?" Emily jumped from her chair and bent to kiss him.

"There, there, child. Watch that fork! Of course I mean it! How could I be such a clodpole? Told you I wasn't in the petticoat line. Can't remember about come outs and things like that. Samantha, you should have reminded me."

In her dismay, Samantha had dropped her spoon. But by the time Porter had retrieved it and brought her another, she was able to achieve a look of tranquility. Not before she had caught Lord Desmond's glance.

Lord Scarborough was deep in plans, as she had known he would be. "My rooms are much too small! Have to lease a house. Lord, I haven't been to Almack's in years. Damme it, Desmond, when does the season begin?"

"In about a month."

"Well, I'll get a letter off to my bankers in the morning. They can start looking for a house."

Now the talk revolved around available housing, possible chaperons and vouchers for Almack's. Emily concentrated on the newest styles, the best dressmakers and the smartest shops. Desmond seemed to have ready answers for both Uncle Stanley and Emily. Samantha and Arthur took no part in the conversation.

Arthur did not remain with the gentlemen, but retired with the ladies to the parlour, where he chided Emily for making such a cake of herself, dangling after Lord Desmond.

"Dangling after him!" Emily retorted. "Why, Arthur Travis, all I did was be polite and gracious, and that was better than sitting stiffly with my mouth shut tight like some people."

This exchange went on for some time, until quite a lively quarrel ensued. Samantha was thankful that the men did not linger over their port and soon joined them.

At their appearance, Emily was all smiles and Arthur took off in a huff, saying politely that he had promised his mama that he would return early.

Emily hardly noticed his going. "London!" she declared, "Oh, I am so excited. I do hope I'll know how to go on and won't appear a green country girl."

"You will do just fine," Lord Desmond assured her.

"But I don't know all the dances. Just the country ones. What is this new dance that Elsie Macom told me about? She was in London last season and says it's all the rage."

"The waltz?"

"Yes, that's it! How does it go?"

Lord Scarborough, who had been engaged in coaxing a brighter blaze from the fire logs, turned around at this, a twinkle in his eye. "You go whirling and whirling around in a gentleman's arms," he said, laughing.

Emily's eyes went wide at the thought of such a provocative dance. "Is it hard to do?"

"Don't look at me," her uncle advised. "Ask the master." He nodded toward his guest.

Emily transferred her gaze to Lord Desmond.

"Much simpler than the minuet or the quadrille," he said, demonstrating. "One, two, three...one, two, three."

"Oh!" Emily clapped her hands. "Let me try. Samantha, play something."

Samantha obliged with music of Desmond's choosing, and the blue coat and dress made a very pretty picture as the partners went swirling about the room. Emily squealed with delight, vowing it was the best dance ever. When at last she fell exhausted on the sofa, Lord Desmond walked over to the spinet and looked down at Samantha. "Your turn."

When Samantha hesitated, Emily cried, "Oh, do, Sam. It's entirely delightful. And you must learn. How goosish we would look if we couldn't do the new dances. Do try."

Samantha loved to dance and was quite as eager as Emily had been to try it. She had watched the two of them and thought it would be easy to follow Desmond. She was not prepared for the tremor of excitement that ran through her as his arms went around her. He held her lightly, but close enough that she was acutely aware of the power and strength of his muscular body. It was like a magnet drawing her to him. She stumbled and he caught her, pulling her even closer.

"Steady there. Sorry. My fault," he said. "There. Just relax and let yourself follow the rhythm. One, two, three...one, two, three...."

She felt flushed and clumsy, and very conscious of that hand on the small of her back. The hand was gently guiding and she willed herself to concentrate on the steps. She did not look up but gazed steadily at his intricately tied cravat. She was a good dancer, graceful and light on her feet. To her surprise, she soon found herself circling about the room, relaxing in a wave of pleasurable excitement that had something to do with the arms that held her, the masculine scent of tobacco and port and the lips so close to her ear that whispered, "One, two, three. One, two three."

So exhilarated was Samantha, so caught up in the dance, that she did not hear Porter's voice in the hall

"I'll announce you, sir."

Nor did she hear the voice that answered.

"Oh, never mind, Porter. I know my way."

At Porter's belated announcement "Sir Malcolm Thomas," the dance came to an abrupt halt. Samantha turned, as surprised to see her would-be suitor as he was to see her in the arms of another man.

"Well, well, good evening, Sir Thomas," Lord Scarborough greeted him. "What brings you about at this late hour?"

"Posies."

"Posies?" Lord Scarborough stared at the late visitor as if trying to fathom his meaning.

"Oh, for Miss Samantha. I was in Hertfordshire this afternoon. I asked Porter to take them up, but he said Miss Samantha was in the parlour. I thought . . . that is—" He seemed a little ill at ease. "I expected to find you abed. Last night, your sister said you were indisposed." He stared fixedly at Samantha.

Becoming aware that Lord Desmond's arms were still around her, Samantha disengaged herself and moved forward. "I was unwell. But I feel much better now. I thank you for the flowers." She took the bouquet from him and begged him to be seated.

A widower of middle years, Sir Malcolm Thomas was not an unhandsome man. He wore his sandy hair rather more close cropped than was the mode and he was a man of modest proportions. There was nothing out of the ordinary about his dark coat and breeches, but his demeanour proclaimed that he was a gentleman of importance.

"This is my friend Lord Mark Desmond," said Lord Scarborough. "And this is Sir Malcolm Thomas, our local squire."

To this introduction and Desmond's smile, Sir Thomas made a perfunctory bow.

Lord Scarborough explained that his nieces were thinking of taking London by storm and Lord Desmond was so kind as to instruct them in the new dance.

"The waltz! It goes like this." Emily seized Desmond and began to demonstrate.

Sir Thomas, who had never seen the waltz, looked his disgust. Thinking to amuse him, Lord Scarborough suggested a game of piquet. The squire said he never played, but Lord Desmond accepted the challenge. The two men sauntered across the room to the table. Emily followed, saying she planned to watch.

This afforded an opportunity for Sir Thomas to speak privately with Samantha. Selecting a seat near her, he spoke confidentially. "I should not presume to choose Lord Scarborough's friends for him."

"Quite right," she answered.

"I beg your pardon?"

"You should not presume to choose his friends."

He was a little taken aback, but pressed on. "But I think he should not bring them here."

"Why not? This is his house."

"But, my dear, you and Emily are his wards."

"Yes. How fortunate we are. He is so very kind."

"Yes, but— My dear, kindness should be tempered with discretion."

"Discretion?"

He bent forward. "Lord Desmond, you know . . . well, of course you wouldn't know. But he has a scandalous reputation, and to expose him to you and Emily is the outside of enough."

"I see," she replied with a laugh. "But do not worry. We will not cast out any lures. I know you mean we are so indiscreet."

"I mean no such thing. Really, Samantha, you have a way of twisting my words. What I mean is—"

"I know what you mean. Pray say no more. He is our guest."

"No, of—of course not," he faltered. "Now what about this London trip? Are you sure it is quite the thing?" He looked across the room at Emily who was evincing a lively interest in the card game by clapping her hands and laughing at every clever play. "Emily, you know, is not like you."

"I know." She sighed. "Pray do not remind me. She walks in beauty."

"Oh, Samantha, I did not mean that. You are quite attractive."

"Thank you," she said, laughing.

"What I mean is—she's so young. So lively. And in London..."

"Oh, yes, I do agree. She is just at an age to enjoy London. With her disposition it would be fatal to keep her in the country. Too dull."

"Oh, no. What I mean is..."

He went on to explain his meaning at such great length that she was thoroughly bored, and glad when tea was brought in. She politely pressed him to stay, but was glad when he declined.

Taking his leave, he said he was happy she was now up to snuff, and since that was the case, would she ride over to take a look at his new foal. He could fetch her in his carriage. "Foal out of Dear Polly," he said. "Sired by Black Knight."

"Colt or filly?" For the first time since he entered the room, Samantha's face showed interest.

"Colt. Quite long legged too. I wish you'd take a look."

"Not tomorrow, but soon," Samantha promised.

After Sir Thomas departed, Lord Desmond surveyed her curiously. "Now why," he asked, "does he want you to take a look at his colt?"

"Because," Stanley answered, "Samantha is the best judge of horse flesh in these parts."

Desmond's eyebrows went up. "Is she, by Jove?"

"She is. And you'd better let her show you around the stables tomorrow. Help you take your pick, plague take it!"

"His pick?" Samantha looked at her uncle.

"Devilish bad run of luck at the dice table, Sam. The thing is, Mark won, and he's here to take his pick of Scarborough Stables."

"Pick of—" Samantha's voice failed her. Her hand was shaking and she put the teacup down very carefully. Her heart was beating fast.

Black Knight! Of course he will pick Black Knight.

CHAPTER FOUR

THE NEXT MORNING, Samantha awoke early as usual. But she had spent a restless night, and her thoughts were still in turmoil. She remembered the sardonic gleam in Lord Desmond's eyes when Uncle Stanley said he was to have the pick of the stable.

Black Knight! He would choose Black Knight.

She remembered the sardonic gleam in Lord Desmond's eyes when Uncle Stanley said he was to have the pick of the stable.

She closed her eyes, recalling her father's words. "He's the one, Samantha. Worth all my years of breeding. He'll be a legend—greater than Eclips, who was his great-great-grandsire. And he'll sire more winners. You mark my words. He and his get will make Scarborough famous."

She brushed away a tear. Papa had not lived to see Black Knight win his first race. He had not yet begun to make his name. And now it would not be Scarborough that he would make famous.

How could Uncle Stanley do this? How could he lose their best to that...that high-staking, plump-in-the-pocket Desmond, who probably had no idea of his real value.

She brushed away a tear, reminding herself that she had no right to call her uncle to cuffs about what he did with his own money or horses. She and Emily were hanging on his sleeve. And now Emily had got her way and they would go to London to spend still more of his money.

But, thought Samantha, innately fair, it was only right that Emily should have the come out she so much wanted. Only why didn't the silly goose marry Arthur, who adored her? Samantha sighed. Emily would never be satisfied until she was dancing at Almack's.

Dancing. Suddenly, unbidden, came the thought of last night's dance. Lord Desmond's arms about her, his lips whispering in her ear, "One, two, three. One, two, three."

Ninnyhammer! It would not be like that in London, and she'd be blue deviled if she kept lying in bed!

She slid from the warm feather bed, and, going to the window, pulled back the blinds and opened the casement. There was a heavy dew and an early morning chill in the air, but no hint of rain. Already the sun was casting its rosy glow over the horizon; a cockerel was strutting in the yard, and a thrush was singing in a nearby tree. A beautiful day for her early morning canter. She heard a shutter slam below and knew her hot chocolate would be waiting. Mrs. Kemper's rule was that Miss Samantha was not to go galloping off without something hot in her stomach.

Samantha reached for her old riding habit and gasped in dismay. She had snagged it on a low-hanging branch yesterday, and, in the rush to get Emily over to Pendleton, had forgot to have it mended. Oh, well, no help for it. She took down the much too fashionable riding habit Uncle Stanley had brought for her birthday. She had worn it only once before. She pulled on the new leather boots, but spurned the feathered hat and veil, simply tying her hair back with a wide green ribbon. Half the pleasure of riding was the wind in her hair and the sun on her face.

Throwing the train of her habit over one arm, her whip in hand, she ran down to the breakfast parlour. On the threshold she paused.

Seated alone at the table, a cup in one hand, the *London Gazette* in the other, was Lord Desmond. She had not expected to see him so early.

As Samantha entered, he put the paper aside and stood. To Samantha, no judge of fashion, his buckskin breeches and buff coat could have been those of any country gentleman. But even her inexperienced eyes could discern the air of ease and elegance with which he wore them.

He stared at her in a slightly quizzical way. He was probably counting her freckles, she thought. Determined not to be abashed, she lifted her head and moved forward, smiling. "Good morning, my lord. Did you sleep well?"

"Very well, thank you. And I see your uncle was right."

"Right?"

"That I'd have to be an early bird to ride with you. Had a notion to try before I buy."

She bent over the chocolate placed before her. No need to ask which horse he'd had saddled.

She was right. In the courtyard, the horse standing beside Sheba, her own grey mare, was Black Knight. She saw Desmond's eyes light up in admiration at sight of the handsome beast, and she felt a little sick.

"He's a heady one, your lordship," Hawkins cautioned as he handed over the reins. "And he ain't an easy seat."

"I know," the marquis said with a laugh, "I've seen him race."

"How is Haro?" Samantha asked the old groom as he helped her into the saddle.

"Fine," he answered. "Getting frisky already. But I've got that leg up so he can't hurt it."

"Good," said Samantha. "I'll get him when we return."

Black Knight reared as Desmond mounted him, but settled down as the marquis spoke softly, holding the reins with calm assurance. Watching the steady hands on the reins, Samantha thought of the way he had guided her through the waltz, taking easy command. He would command Black Knight just as easily, she thought. That was too bad. The only hope she had of keeping the prized stallion was that Desmond could not control him. Now that hope was gone.

Samantha's instinctive admiration for expert horsemanship was overcome by dread at the thought of losing Black Knight. In a mingled flash of annoyance and anger, she gave Sheba an uncharacteristically sharp flick with her riding crop. The horse bolted across the lawn toward the open meadow. A startled Lord Desmond galloped in pursuit.

It was several miles before Samantha slowed her pace. As always, the morning chill and the wind racing through her hair had a calming effect. Samantha had not had a companion on her morning rides since her father died. Emily was not addicted to horses and still less to early hours. It was good to have someone racing with her.

Well, they were not exactly racing. Black Knight could have easily outdistanced her Sheba, but Desmond held him back, keeping pace with her. Samantha noted how easily he took the hedges, never cramming his horse.

They had had quite a run by the time they reached the stream, where the horses fell into an easy trot. Possibly out of habit, Sheba stopped altogether.

Lord Desmond reined in Black Knight and dismounted. He strolled over to Samantha, and, before she could take his arm, took her about the waist and handily lifted her down. Once again she was keenly conscious of his strength.

He did not release her immediately, but stood looking down at her. "Have I in some way offended you, Miss Scarborough?"

Totally unprepared for the question, Samantha could only stammer that of course he had not.

"Then what do you hold against me? Has my scandalous reputation preceded me?"

"No. Well, yes," she answered, incurably honest. "But of course I don't hold that against you."

"Thank you."

"Well, what I mean is, a man has a right to any reputation he . . . well, that is—to live in any way he chooses."

"Spoken like a lady with a strong sense of justice. Still, it puts me in somewhat of a puzzle." He produced two lumps of sugar from his pocket and fingered them thoughtfully. "If I have not offended you, and you kindly concede my right to my reputation, why have you taken me in such dislike?"

He had turned his back to her and was feeding the sugar to the horses. Samantha was glad he could not see her face, for she was sure it was hot and flushed. Why, indeed, should she dislike him? It was not his fault.

"I—I am sorry. It is not you. There are other circumstances. That is, I—I did not mean to be uncivil. You have been nothing but kind. Pray forgive me."

He came toward her now, smiling and dusting his hands. "Nothing to forgive. And I cannot blame you for being cautious. My kindness could be a facade. Wolf in sheep's clothing, you know."

"Now you are funning with me."

"Indeed I am not. A rake shows many faces to the world. Everyone does, for that matter. Even you."

"Me?"

"Yes, indeed. That was definitely a hoyden who stopped my horses on the road. Last night saw a prim governess." He surveyed her critically. "Now you present me with a lady in the first style of elegance."

She laughed then, looking down at the plush velvet skirt. "I know. But there's no convincing Uncle that the clothes he brings us are too grand for the country. Can you see me traipsing about the stables in this?" She picked up the train of her habit and gave a little turn. "At least I didn't wear the fancy hat with the plume and veil."

"Good. For it would have been a pity to cover up that hair."

Emily would have giggled in appreciation. But, totally unused to such compliments and scarcely believing what she heard, Samantha could only turn toward the brook and stammer that this was her favourite spot in all the county.

"Does anyone ever fish here?" Desmond asked, looking at the abundance of trout that flitted through the clear turbulent water.

"Papa and I used to. I once caught a fish that big." She extended her hands.

"Not you?"

"Yes, I. And don't make a face like Mrs. Kemper. I know you think that ladies should not fish and—"

"No, no, I simply wondered that you, of all people, could bear to have a poor little fish squirming on the end of your hook."

She glanced up. "Now you are teasing."

"I assure you I am not. For a lady who abhors fox hunting—"

"Oh, but that is different."

"How is it different?"

"Well, for one thing, there are hundreds of fish and just one hook. Lots of juicy worms, too. So it's just a matter of luck which fish encounters the worm on my hook. Oh, you needn't laugh. It is different from trying to corner one poor little frightened fox. There he goes, scampering all across the countryside trying to find a place to hide. And there are all those hounds baying and all those people on horses running after him and blowing horns and shouting tallyho. It's dreadful."

"My dear lady, your attitude is most un-English."

"Well, I can't help it. I deplore fox hunting. It—it's not good sportsmanship."

"Well, my dear, it is an English tradition—like horse racing," Desmond said, a devilish gleam in his eyes.

"I do not dislike horse racing."

"That's right. You just disapprove of springing one's horses for too long on a crowded highway."

"Yes, but not only that. Races should be regulated so that everything is fair and the horses are properly treated. You know there are quite a few disreputable racetracks."

"Oh? And how do you know about them?"

"Papa took me with him to almost all of them."

"Ascot?"

"No, I've never been there. Papa said that sooner or later the best horses always came to Newmarket, and we were always there for the Tattersall sales. Papa was more interested in breeding horses than racing them, and he was very clever at that."

"Yes. The Scarborough Stables have gained a remarkable reputation. So you went with your father?"

"Yes, though Mrs. Kemper was always scolding him for treating me like the boy he never had."

"Did he?"

"I suppose so. But I loved it. I loved going to the sales and I loved being in the stables and fishing and . . ."

"You miss him, don't you?"

"So much. Sometimes he would have Cook pack a lunch, and we'd come and sit right here." She sat on a fallen tree trunk and gave it an affectionate pat. "We'd talk and fish sometimes for hours. Yes, I miss him."

"What about your Uncle Stanley?"

"He—he likes different things."

"Yes, very different." He picked up a stone and sent it skimming across the water.

"Oh, but he is the very best of uncles," she said quickly. "So good humoured. And so kind. Eager to do anything that would please us."

"And London *don't* please you?" he asked, sitting beside her.

"No, it's not that." She hesitated. "Well, it would be good for Emily. I've already been, you know."

"And you didn't like it."

She shook her head. "Not very much."

"Not Almack's?"

"Especially not Almack's." She was quite vehement, remembering. "I felt like a filly waiting with a bunch of other fillies to be auctioned off. All preening and bowing and holding out their dance cards, and I..." She stopped, realizing that he was convulsed with laughter. "I'm sorry. I didn't mean it. I shouldn't have said that."

"On the contrary," he said between gasps of laughter. "I have never heard Almack's so aptly described."

She considered. "No, I daresay I only felt that way because I was out of place. I am persuaded Emily will like it immensely."

"So will you, my dear."

She looked at him, doubt in her eyes.

"Pale blond tresses are tuppence a dozen in London. Just wait until Monsieur Maurice gets his scissors into those copper curls of yours."

As she continued to stare at him, speechless, he smiled and shook his head. "With hair that dances in the sunlight and eyes of liquid jade... Dear me, Miss Samantha Scarborough, is it possible that you are unaware of your unusual beauty?"

Her eyes widened and her hand flew automatically to her nose.

He took her hand away and held it in his own. "Don't cover them up. I find them entrancing."

"My—my freckles?"

"Yes." He examined her closely. "All six of them."

"Only six? Is that all? Mrs. Kemper said they would fade away but I..."

"I hope they won't all fade away. I like them."

"You're roasting me!"

"More like flirting than roasting, my dear."

"Flirting? Were you flirting with me? Was I casting out lures?"

"Casting—casting out lures?" His shoulders began to shake again, and it was some time before he could answer. "No. No, my dear, I assure you that asking me to count your freckles is not casting out lures!"

"No, I suppose not. The thing is, Mrs. Kemper is always warning me not to, and I am—I am always promising not to. But, to own the truth, I should not at all know how to go about it."

"Don't ever learn," he said quite soberly, though the laughter remained in his eyes. "And don't worry. I was not flirting. Only telling you a few truths which you obviously did not know. Though why you have not been told before puts me in quite a puzzle."

She looked at him, not at all sure what he meant.

"Never mind, dear lady. Despite conflicting rumours, I remember that I was bred a gentleman. I was not flirting." He looked down at her, a teasing glint in his eyes. "Now if you were the hoyden I first took you for ... But I do not dally with ladies of quality. You are quite safe. Come."

Samantha had time to show Desmond the stables and training grounds before noon. He was particularly impressed with the area that had been marked for clocking the horses and the area where Hawkins stood with a couple of grooms, testing three of the mares.

"Why," Desmond asked, "does he watch them from the top of that hill?"

"Oh, that's the best way to inspect their legs—to get an idea of their strength," Samantha explained, excitement and pride in her voice, as always when she talked about the workings of Scarborough. "An innovation of Papa's. The clocking area was his idea, too. Papa was very clever."

"Like father, like daughter," he murmured, but she hardly heard him.

Her gaze followed the little chestnut mare that was at that moment climbing the hill. "Look. That's Dainty Lady out of Lady Be Good by Bluebeard. Look at those legs. She's going to be a great jumper. Or we might race her next season. Isn't she a beauty?"

"She is, indeed," agreed Desmond, but he was not looking at the mare.

Samantha gave him a thorough tour, showing him the breeding area, the foaling pens and the sturdy separate stalls which housed the stallions.

"Very impressive. Very impressive," Desmond kept saying.

He had Clinton, his groom, accompany them when he began to inspect the horses. Well versed in the lineage of every horse in the stable, Samantha stressed the excellent qualities and potential of every possible choice, but she was well aware that Desmond knew Black Knight was the top of the line.

However, the marquis did seem very interested in the bay mares, and commented particularly upon the markings of Bonnie. Bonnie was a beautiful bay colour, with the typical dark legs, mane and tail, and after Black Knight, she was Samantha's favourite.

Desmond studied the mare closely, even asking Clinton to measure her.

"Sixteen hands exactly, my lord. Very good match," Clinton reported. Then, thinking himself unobserved by Samantha, he ventured in a low voice, "Begging your pardon, my lord. She's a beauty and a good match and all. But, lord, sir, when would you get another chance at a stallion like Black Knight?"

When would he indeed, Samantha thought, and knew she had little reason to hope.

CHAPTER FIVE

BY THE TIME THEY LEFT the stable, the clear skies of the morning had been darkened by clouds and there was a sharp breeze. It was going to rain, after all.

The dark clouds were much in keeping with Samantha's mood, and she found herself unable to enjoy the elaborate meal Cook had prepared. Emily was in gayest mood and kept Desmond busy answering all her questions. Samantha toyed with her baked fish and watched her uncle across the table. He ate heartily and seemed not to have a care in the world beyond advising Emily that no, he thought ermine, not sable, was a better trim for a blue evening cloak.

How could he be so calm?

On her tour of the stables, Samantha had become particularly aware of the number of empty stalls. Scarborough was being drained of the fine stallions which were it's lifeblood. And Simmons had had to dig into the capital. If Uncle Stanley kept on like this he'd soon not have a feather to fly with. She had to talk with him, try to make him understand.

She knew the two men were leaving tomorrow morning and almost despaired of gaining a private audience with her uncle. But, soon after nuncheon, she encountered him in the hall. Taking his arm, she drew him quickly into the library.

This large room was a favourite family retreat with its many windows and easy access to the garden. Now, though the promised rain pelted against the windows, there was a log fire blazing in the big open hearth, and the room was warm and inviting.

Samantha shut the door and faced Lord Scarborough. "Uncle, I must speak with you."

"Of course, child. Don't look so worried. No need to tease yourself. I know you'll be needing new clothes for London. Matter of fact, I was thinking that we should—"

"Uncle, I do not want to talk about London. That is, I do. But—well, there's something else."

"All right, Puss. Come over here and sit, and we'll have a cosy chat." He started toward the oversize sofa placed directly in front of the fire.

Samantha pulled him back, leading him instead to the desk by the window. Perhaps if they both took a look at the account books which were stacked there she could make him understand the gravity of the situation. "Simmons asked me to speak with you."

"Simmons! That clutch-fisted old fussbudget! Has he been pestering you, too?"

"No, not pestering. He is just concerned. He says we are in pretty desperate financial straits."

"Devil take the fellow! The gudgeon is bothering you with what don't concern you. These matters are not for you to worry your pretty little head about. Dash it, Sam, I've a notion to turn the fellow off!"

"No, you can't do that! He's been bailiff here for years."

"Oh, no, of course I wouldn't turn him off. But it's plain as a pikestaff! Fellow's a purse pincher. Tell you what, Sam, I don't think the sapskull ever saw a dun in his life. Pretty night fainted when he got my bill from Weston."

"Yes, Uncle, but—"

"Thing is, Weston's devilish high. But ain't nothing like the fit of his coats. Pierce can't touch him. Where's my snuff?'' He searched his pocket and produced the small gold box. "Special mixture, Sam. Nut brandy. Taylor mixes it for me.''

"Please, Uncle Stanley, do listen.''

"I'm listening. I'm listening.'' He took a pinch of snuff and held it to one nostril.

"Simmons told me—''

"Plague take Simmons! That stiff-necked old pigeon is getting downright senile. Worrying a child like you. Take no heed of him. Leave everything to me.'' He snapped the box shut and returned it to his pocket.

In desperation, Samantha seized the lapels of Weston's well-cut coat. "Listen, Uncle Stanley. Today I found that five of our best stallions are gone. And also some of the mares.''

"Oh, I know what's bothering you. You don't want Desmond to take Black Knight. And he will, plague take his luck.'' He touched her hand tenderly. "I hate that, Sam. I really do. But there wasn't nothing like the run of the luck that night. Never threw one number that I called. Desmond was holding the bank—must have been four thousand in it. I threw him for it, staking the pick of my stable since I was clean out of the ready. Dash it, Sam, that Desmond's a lucky dog. But you know I can't go back on my word. Debt of honour, you know.''

"It's not just Black Knight,'' Samantha cried in frustration. "It's everything! With the best stallions gone, there go the stud fees which Simmons counts on to supplement the rents. And there goes our breeding programme, too.''

"Damme it, Sam. Now you're talking like a common horse trader. You just concentrate on getting yourself ready for London!''

"That's another thing. Perhaps we shouldn't go to London.''

"Not go to London!" He looked at her as if she had lost her senses. "You have to go to London!"

"Why?"

"Well, because it's the thing. Everyone does, you know."

"Why?"

"Lord, child. I don't know. Almack's—town polish—that kind of thing. George'd never forgive me if I didn't take you. Emily's on her head to go, and I thought you were, too, Samantha."

"But it's so frightfully expensive to hire a house and staff."

"Oh, there you go again about what don't concern you. Those are my problems."

"I have it," Samantha said, wondering why the idea had not occurred to her before. "We can use my jointure to finance the London trip."

"Samantha, as if I would do such a thing!"

"But," she faltered, seeing the stricken look on his face, "the trip is for Emily and myself. And that's what the money is for, isn't it?"

"It is not. It is your independence, to be taken with you when you marry."

"But if we choose to use it now—"

"We do not choose to use it now. You're under my protection until you marry. And I would not cast you on a husband without your own means. You know some husbands can be devilish clutch-fisted! I bet Mrs. Simmons hasn't had a new hat in three years."

"Uncle!"

"You know, Sam, I was planning to travel with Desmond. But I think I'd better take my own chaise and go on up to London. See about that house. And I better go up now and tell Robert to pack enough things for London."

"Uncle, please listen."

"Now everything is settled. You are not to let Simmons pester you. Get yourself ready. Matter of fact, I think you and Emily should go up early, too. Get that Monsieur what's-his-name to do your hair. And do some shopping."

"We don't need to shop."

"Now, now. Can't go to Almack's in rags, you know. Must get to Robert now. Glad we had this little talk, Sam. Good to clear the air now and then."

He went out, leaving a baffled Samantha staring disconsolately at the untouched account books. She had had her talk, and what good had it done?

Completely thwarted, she stalked across the room. In a mounting wave of fury and frustration, she seized the poker and stabbed viciously at the fire logs.

Dear kind, generous, lovable, stupid, foolish, reckless, ungovernable...

A discreet cough startled her. She turned to see a sheepish Lord Desmond rising from the sofa. "You!" she exclaimed in disbelief. "How could you? Of all the sneaking, conniving, despicable things to do!"

"Now just be calm, Miss Scarborough. Compose yourself!" He was staring not at her, but at something over her right shoulder.

Following his gaze, she saw the upraised poker poised threateningly in her hand. She lowered it, feeling a hysterical desire to laugh. Or cry. She was not sure which. "How could you?" she whispered. "You were—you were eavesdropping."

"Acquit me, dear lady. That was not my intention."

"Eavesdropping!" she repeated. "And I am persuaded it was your intention."

"Now really, Miss Scarborough. You do me an injustice."

"Otherwise," she said, "you would have discovered yourself to us."

"But it would have been exceedingly awkward. You see, I was in the middle of it before I knew it. I was asleep, you see, and it was the discussion which—er—awakened me."

She said nothing, but somehow, beneath the anger and confusion, the logic of his words began to penetrate.

"I thought it best just to lie here quietly until you went away. I didn't expect you to come charging over here, fighting the fire."

"You are abominable!" she retorted. "Now it is all my fault."

"Well, yes." He rubbed the back of his neck and stifled a yawn. "As a matter of fact, it was your fault."

"Oh! Just because I walked into my own library."

"No. Not that. It was your unprecedented and ungodly tendency to go riding before dawn. It quite undid me. Just slipped in here after nuncheon to—to recover."

Again there was that uncontrollable feeling between tears and laughter. She felt her lips begin to quiver.

"There, that's better. There's that dimple." He walked over, took the poker from her and replaced it in its stand. "Come. Let us endeavour to work ourselves out of this muddle."

"Ourselves?" Though she allowed him to lead her to the sofa, she could not resist saying that the muddle was no concern of his and if he were a gentleman, he would banish from his mind the whole conversation.

"That was a conversation? All I heard you say was 'Uncle, listen.'"

His realization of her frustration triggered another flash of annoyance, and Samantha started to rise.

He caught her hand, restraining her. "Now wait, Samantha. As I told you, we shall endeavour to remedy our situations."

"*Our* situations?" So puzzled was she by his statement that she failed to notice the familiar use of her name.

"Yes. I'm in a bit of a muddle myself," he admitted.

CHAPTER SIX

SAMANTHA STUDIED Desmond's face. What possible problem could this controlled strong-willed man have? "You?" she asked. "You have some difficulty?"

"Not so much a difficulty as a desire," he countered.

"Desire?"

"To live as I choose. You did say I had that right."

"Of course."

"Well, I don't choose to be leg shackled."

"Leg shackled?"

"Married!"

"But that seems easy to avoid."

"You don't know my mother and her unrelenting determination to attach me to some female of the first respectability."

For a moment Samantha simply looked at him. Then she began to laugh, wildly, helplessly. The laughter was a release, bursting the bubble of pent-up tension within her. When at last she became relatively calm, she looked up to find Desmond staring at her in surprise.

"You find that amusing?"

"It's only," she stammered, "that your repu—that is, rumour has it that you're always attached to some female."

"But not one of the first respectability," he defended himself.

"Oh," she said soberly, quite unaware of the telltale dimple lurking at the corner of her mouth. "Forgive me.

It was just that the picture of your avoiding an entanglement quite overcame me."

"Yes. I can see that it did," he said drily. "You may laugh. But it can be damned awkward." He stood up and began to pace in front of her. "Ordinarily, I can absent myself. But I promised this season to be... Oh, never mind all that." He stopped pacing and stood in front of her, hands in his pockets. "It is indeed fortunate, Miss Scarborough, that I overheard your conversation. For I have hit upon a scheme whereby we both may be mutually served."

Stunned with surprise, she listened while he unfolded his plan. If he were to tell his mother that he was thinking of offering for the hand of Miss Samantha Scarborough, the duchess would be induced to invite Samantha and her sister to visit at her London town house during the season, thereby eliminating the expense of house, servants and chaperon. Samantha's presence would protect Desmond from any other prospective brides his mother had in mind.

In her direct way, Samantha asked the first question that came to mind. "Why on earth should your mother feel impelled to invite us?"

"Because, my dear, you are the niece of the late Agatha Sandford Weatherby, of the Sandfords of Havenside. Lady Weatherby was my mother's dearest friend when they both were students at Mrs. Pinkerton's Academy for Young Ladies—a fact she has often mentioned to your Uncle Stanley. In other words, Miss Scarborough, you are exactly what my mother has in mind for me. A lady—"

"Of the first respectability!" she finished for him.

"Exactly."

Samantha stood up, and for a moment looked down into the fire. Then she turned to face him. "I think not."

"Why not?"

"It's—it's dishonest. I dislike deceiving your parents."

"You are not deceiving them. For all you know I may be thinking of offering for you."

She glanced at him suspiciously. He gave his neckcloth a nervous twitch. "Anyway, I am not saying we are betrothed. That leaves you free to choose among the many suitors who are sure to offer for you."

"Suppose none offer or I do not choose," said the practical Samantha.

"Then I offer and you refuse, leaving me broken-hearted but free for at least another season."

Samantha could not immediately agree to such a preposterous scheme, but she did agree to think it over. That night, as she tossed in her bed, she admitted that it would spare Uncle Stanley the costs of the London trip. And, after all, what harm could it do?

Morning held a surprise! Desmond had *not* chosen Black Knight!

"He took the bay mare, Bonnie. Said he had a special need for her," Lord Scarborough explained. "And Desmond suggested—I wonder I hadn't thought of it myself—that I make a present of Black Knight to you. So I had Simmons draw up the papers. There now." He gave her a kiss on the forehead. "He's safe. You never need to worry that I'll gamble him away. That ease your mind a little?"

It did ease her mind, and put her in such charity with Lord Desmond that when he took her hand upon leaving and asked, "Shall I speak with my mother?" she agreed that he might.

THREE WEEKS LATER, in her cheerful withdrawing room overlooking Grosvenor Square, her grace, the duchess of Duval, greeted her sister with joyful news. "Mark has finally chosen his true love."

"Oh, no, Sylvia. How dreadful!" Resplendent in purple velvet, Lady Julia Marlowe laid aside her reticule and gloves and prepared to sympathize.

"Dreadful?" the duchess gasped. This was hardly the response she expected.

"Really, Sylvia, an actress! It's too bad! Surely he can be persuaded against it."

"Actress? Whatever are you talking about?"

"Jasper saw him with her last night. He was late leaving the theatre and he saw that natty tilbury of Mark's parked near the stage door. Jasper started over to speak, but then that D'Angelo woman came out and joined Mark. Well, of course Jasper turned back. He had Melissa with him and could on no account allow her to speak with such a person. So when you said that Mark had—"

"Oh, don't be ridiculous, Julia! Surely you must know that Mark could not be serious about one of those—those muslin skirts."

"Oh, I'm so relieved to hear you say that." Lady Marlowe sat down and spread her hands to the fire. "It was—well, Jasper said they seemed so friendly. And when you said that Mark was betrothed, well, naturally, I . . ."

"Oh, Jasper must know that Mark only amuses himself with such company." The duchess's taffeta skirt ruffled as she gave an exasperated turn. It was true that Jasper Marlowe was a sensible young man who had already married that insipid Melissa and properly presented his widowed mother with three grandchildren. But he was a bit of a prosey and certainly an inveterate tale bearer.

"Mark's chosen one is a lady. One of the Sandfords. Do you remember Agatha Sandford? She was at Miss Pinkerton's Academy with me."

"Agatha Weatherby?"

"Yes, she married that horrid Sir Lionel Weatherby, who was supposed to be such a grand catch! Rumoured to be one of the warmest men in England. But it turned out he had only that house in Berkeley Square and a very mean income! He died a year after they married, leaving poor Agatha with hardly enough to sustain herself. Thank goodness they had no children!"

"But I thought you said her daughter—"

"Oh, not her daughter. Her niece." Her grace seated herself in a chair across from her sister. "Evelyn Sandford was much prettier than Agatha. Such golden hair! And the biggest of blue eyes! Anyway, she married George Scarborough, and they had two girls. It's their eldest daughter, Samantha, whom Mark has chosen. Both the girls are arriving this very afternoon for a visit. And I'm so glad. Such a relief!" She drew a handkerchief from her pocket and daintily patted her face. "I was so dreading this season with Eliza Campbell bringing out her daughter Kate."

"Really, Sylvia—that was the most scatterbrained scheme!"

"It wasn't my scheme. But Eliza is my dearest friend, and what could I do when she kept hinting and hinting..."

"Well, you must have had more hair than wit to suppose that you could interest Mark in little Kate Campbell. Not that she's so little anymore! And quite plain! Really, Sylvia, when you know how Mark is addicted to beauties!"

"Yes, I do know," her sister agreed. "That's why it's so wonderful that Mark has finally chosen for himself!"

"He has not chosen, my dear." His grace, the duke of Duval, leaning heavily on a cane, entered the room in time to hear his wife's last words. He turned to his sister-in-law. "His missive clearly stated that he was only thinking of offering for the lady."

"Oh, what does that signify?" His wife got up and placed a footstool near her lord's favourite chair. "Here, dearest. Rest that leg. Is it feeling better?"

"Much better. Thank you, my dear." The duke eased himself into the chair, carefully placing his left leg on the footstool. "How are you, Julia?"

"Very well, Duval. And remind me before I leave. I brought a copy of Dr. Franklin's vegetable diet for the gout and digestive disorders. You might try it."

"Might as well." The duke took up his book and opened it. "I've tried everything else. Thoughtful of you, Julia."

Lady Marlowe turned to her sister. "Now, what is this about Mark? Is he engaged or isn't he?"

"Well, not exactly," the duchess confessed, glancing at her lord. "But I'm persuaded he is only waiting for my approval."

The duke raised dark expressive eyes, so like his son's, from his book, but said nothing.

His lady pointed a finger at him. "And you needn't look at me like that, sir. Mark's very words, just before he left, were 'Shall I bring the lady for your inspection?' Of course I thought he was only funning. But naturally he wants my approval. And he shall have it, the dear boy! Agatha Sandford's niece! He couldn't have made a better choice!"

CHAPTER SEVEN

ONE, TWO, THREE. One, two, three.

But she didn't need to count anymore. The lively waltz tempo was carried by the lilting strains of the four violins, and Samantha's satin-clad feet sped across the polished ballroom floor in perfect time to the magic rhythm. She wore a sea-green ball gown of gossamer silk trimmed with seed pearls. Its shimmering folds swirled about her as she dipped and swayed to the music.

With Desmond's arms around her, Samantha was only barely conscious of the throng of men and women in colourful evening dress who danced to the same tune. Great mounds of flowers were banked against the walls amid towering candelabras. The flickering candles cast their pale light indiscriminately on the dancers, the darting bows of the violinists, and the dowagers who sat smiling and gossiping. The whole scene was reflected in the oversize mirror on the back wall.

One, two, three. One, two, three.

It was like being in a dream, enchanting, intoxicating, as refreshing as a morning ride on Sheba.

"I told you that you would like it."

Samantha's heart gave a thud as she looked up to meet Desmond's smiling eyes. She had not yet grown accustomed to that smile, the way his gaze seemed to caress her, not yet to the thrill of his touch. But she had learned to control her response. Her feet never missed a beat, and there was not a quiver in her voice as she answered him.

"Yes. And I do like it. So sweet of your parents to give this ball for us. But I do feel a little guilty."

"You needn't. My mother loves to entertain. She uses any excuse to do so."

The music had stopped now, and he led her to a seat in a small alcove. Samantha looked up at him and wondered, as she had many times before, how a man could be at once so careless and yet so distinguished in appearance. Never one to overburden himself with the appurtenances and jewels sported by the tulips of fashion, even now he wore only his signet ring and one splendid sapphire nestled among the folds of his cravat. He was the handsomest man in the room!

Samantha was acutely aware of the number of envious feminine eyes that had marked their progress across the room and were now covertly watching them. If they only knew, she thought. *All a farce. All pretence.*

Desmond touched her chin lightly with his finger, tilting her face upward. "Dear me! Only four left!"

"Four?"

"Freckles, my love. What a pity!"

"Wretch!" She brushed his hand away with her fan. "Just when I was beginning to feel beautiful!"

"Well, don't despair. The eyes are still huge and more lovely than ever. Perhaps you should always wear green. And I do believe your hair sparkles in candlelight, as well."

Samantha felt her pulse quicken. She fanned herself vigorously with the small ivory fan, hoping its green plumes would hide her flushed face.

"It is rather warm," he said. "I'll get you some punch."

She watched him depart, reminding herself again that this was all a sham. Sometimes she almost forgot. Everything seemed so real. From the very first moment—the warm welcome extended by the duke and duchess—she had felt almost as if she were already their daughter-in-law and that they were well pleased with her.

The duchess had seized Emily eagerly. "I knew it. I knew it. So much like your mother, child. The same hair! And those same big blue eyes! Samantha, my dear, I'm so glad—"

"No, Mother, this is Samantha."

The duchess had turned quickly at her son's words. If she were disappointed, Samantha thought, she hid it very well.

She embraced Samantha warmly, telling her she was a dear to come. How wonderful that they were to have the chance to become intimate so soon. Of course she thought they were already dearest friends. Their poor darling Aunt Agatha and she had been friends for so many years, ever since— Oh, my goodness, so long ago. Such silly unruly girls they had been and what tricks they had played on poor Miss Pinkerton. Oh, my, they must have had a tiresome trip. But there would be time to rest and refresh themselves before dinner. And, oh my, what a delightful time they would have. So many parties. So many plans. She'd never had a daughter, you know. And just one son. "But of course he's very special. I'm sure you know that, Samantha. So handsome and so dependable. Couldn't ask for better—but you know how sons are. How nice to have two beautiful daughters to take shopping and driving and to the milliners and to balls." Such fun they would have.

When his lady paused for breath, the duke also received them very graciously. Didn't care much for balls with his goutish leg, but he liked to hear about them, and what a lift it would give the house to have two lively lovely girls in it.

Though a bit overwhelmed, the girls certainly felt welcome. Samantha was glad Uncle Stanley had remembered their hosts in his own inimitable fashion: a rich sable muff for the duchess and a handsome embossed snuff box for the duke.

Lord Stanley did not forget his girls, either. First, he insisted, an appointment with Monsieur Maurice.

The little Frenchman looked them over carefully before he began. He walked around, studied them, tilted their faces this way and that, murmuring in his native tongue.

Emily had brought the sketch from *Modes and Manners* and monsieur looked at it, then nodded approvingly. "À la russe." Then, with deft hands, he went to work, enhancing the copy with his own unique touches and achieving a masterpiece far outweighing Jenny's poor attempt.

However, not one movement of the skilful hands had escaped Jenny's watchful eyes. For they had brought her with them, after all. Lord Scarborough had insisted. "You cannot expect the duke's servants to take care of your personal needs."

Samantha knew that Jenny would be able to duplicate Monsieur Maurice's hairstyles—her own as well as Emily's.

The little coiffeur went into raptures over Samantha's hair. "Such colour! Such fire! But not brazen, more like a subdued flame!"

His scissors snipped away and a different Samantha emerged. A Samantha with a burnished row of ringlets cascading from the top of her head to her shoulders in carefully arranged carelessness.

"I knew he could do it!" Lord Desmond exclaimed when he saw her, and Samantha thought he was pleased. But then he added, "The same effect as on the day I first saw you."

Well, that was ridiculous, for her hair had not been arranged at all on that day.

Desmond had turned away murmuring something that sounded like "hoydenish with a ladylike touch." But she could not be sure.

Then there was the shopping. Hours of it, in modish salons with lots of mirrors, deep carpets and gilded chairs. Samantha quailed at the elegant setting. Surely anything here must be too dear.

But Lord Scarborough, who supervised all their shopping, never asked a price. He seemed only concerned that they should have enough outfits for every occasion. When Emily hesitated between a morning dress of blue poplin or one in muslin, he waved a hand. "Take them both, child. They suit you."

In fact, that was his only criterion. That it suited. With unerring good taste, he chose what was best for Emily's buxom figure and what would enhance Samantha's diminutive one.

He was very definite about colours. Lilacs, blues and lavender for Emily. Rich golds, greens and deep red for Samantha.

He was exacting, authoritative. He rejected with a wave of his hand what he did not approve. No, not the black velvet cloak which Emily preferred. "Take the blue with the ermine trim and muff. Samantha, you try that cherry-red ruched with satin."

Samantha wanted to stop him, to question about money. But there seemed no opportunity. And nobody seemed to care.

Shopkeepers moved with alacrity in response to Lord Scarborough's demands. "Yes, sir, no, sir, would you like this, your lordship?" Surely they would not be so obsequious if they doubted his ability to pay.

Samantha began to think as Emily did. Perhaps Simmons had exaggerated. Perhaps it had been foolish of her to worry over the expense of hiring a house and servants. Certainly there were no clouds on Uncle Stanley's brow. She watched him now, laughing and talking with Lady Marlowe and the duke. He was as elegant as ever in his powder-blue evening coat. As Samantha watched, he and his two companions turned toward the room where the card tables were set up. There, she knew, they would play at faro or basset for exceedingly high stakes, and Lord Scarborough would win or lose with the same air of careless ease.

Somehow that ease had transmitted itself to Samantha. Under the spell of her uncle's extravagance and faultless taste, she succumbed to the lure of the many exquisite dresses and bonnets.

Though she was a sensible and sober girl, not much given to vanity, her young girl's heart could not help but delight in her new appearance. No longer was she an awkward schoolgirl, hiding her freckles and blushing for her inadequacies. She knew, of course, that she was no beauty. But the burnished copper curls à la Monsieur Maurice and the frivolous finery of her uncle's providing somehow produced a sparkle and charm more entrancing than mere prettiness.

Then there was the added security of entering a ballroom on the arm of the handsome and most eligible Lord Desmond and of receiving his rapt and full attention.

The once abhorred routs and balls now seemed delightful. Between them, the shopping expeditions and the theatre parties, Samantha rotated ecstatically, as if floating on billowy clouds of pure pleasure. Yesterday's tension and mundane concerns faded into nothingness, and she gave herself up to the joy of the moment.

There had been a twinge of guilt, however, when she saw the elaborate preparations being made for this particular ball. Desmond might attribute it to his mother's partiality for entertaining, but Samantha knew that the duchess was hoping to make an announcement. Her grace seemed to accept this pretended betrothal as fact, and was all but making preparations for the marriage. Samantha blushed under her conspiratorial glances; she didn't know how to answer her leading questions.

Now she glanced across the room at her hostess. Modishly attired in rose taffeta trimmed with deep ruffles of Aleçon lace, a tiny tiara in her silver streaked golden hair, the duchess looked very beautiful and very happy. She was talking animatedly to a plump dowager in purple satin and, with a flip of her hand, directed the lady's gaze first to Samantha and then to Lord Desmond. Samantha felt herself blush as she imagined what the duchess was saying.

She was not far from wrong.

"Of course, it is not a settled thing," the duchess imparted to her dearest friend, Eliza Campbell. "No, not a word. Mark kept very mum. We knew nothing until about three weeks ago, and of course the dear boy wanted me to meet her before... Well, what could I do? He asked me to have them down for the season and— What? Scarborough, Samantha Scarborough. You remember Agatha Weatherby? Sandford, she was, of the Sandfords of Havenside. Yes. At Miss Pinkerton's. No, her niece. You remember her sister, Evelyn. Yes. George Scarborough. Horses?" Her grace gave her nose a nervous pat with a rose handkerchief delicately edged with lace. "Oh, my dear, no. That was only a hobby. He was interested in bloodlines and breeding, I think. That sort of thing. Yes, a year ago. The property went to his brother. You know, Lord Stanley Scarborough. Well, yes, it was—quite a surprise. You know the plans you and I were making..." She touched Lady Campbell's arm. "Well, the best laid plans of mothers often go awry. You know how these children are. Oh, my dear, Kate does look darling—so virginal in all that white." *All those ruffles,* she thought privately, *Eliza should have had better sense!* Poor child. She looked so uncomfortable, standing all alone. Now there was Samantha with Mark, joining her.

"Samantha's such a dear. So friendly," she said aloud. Samantha did have a knack for picking out any girl who seemed lonely and unhappy and making her comfortable, the duchess mused. So thoughtful of her, when she was so popular herself. Now Samantha was calling that boy—what was his name? He had come down from the country soon after they had. Taylor? No, Travis, Arthur Travis.

The duchess saw Lady Campbell's eyes light up as the young man bent over her daughter's hand. "Travis. Arthur Travis," she said in answer to the lady's question. "Neighbours of the Scarboroughs. Sir John Travis. Oh, yes, I think. Very well-to-do. Oh, yes, I would think—quite eligible."

Lady Campbell took up her quizzing glass and focused it on Arthur.

Arthur felt his own quizzing glass bump against the new snuffbox in the pocket of his weskit as he bent over the young lady. Transferring his fan from his right to his left hand, he executed a very creditable bow, not quite allowing his lips to touch the pudgy hand extended to him.

Why the devil had Samantha called him, anyway? Just as he was about to get next to Emily. Well, he would have been if that Lord—Lord—well, whatever his name was—the one with the green coat and all those rings on his fingers—hadn't cut in front of him. And there was Emily, smiling up at old-rings-on-his-finger as if he were a god or something.

What a ninny Emily was! Sitting there in that gauzy lilac thing like she was a duchess herself, tossing her hair and smirking and smiling at every man who looked her way. Except him. Not once had she looked at him.

And he had taken such pains. He knew he was all the go. His short velvet coat was decorated with frog buttons. He wore a flowered weskit and breeches of white satin striped in blue with lots of strings at the knees. He had on several rings, and big diamond buckles graced his shoes.

He had pictured himself matched with and escorting a blue-gowned Emily to dine. But Emily was not wearing blue. She was wearing lilac. Now it looked as if he would not get near her before supper, Arthur thought unhappily as he scrawled his name on Miss Kate Campbell's dance card.

Having assured herself that this forlorn girl would have a partner for at least one dance, Samantha stepped back to find herself surrounded by several gentlemen. Two were requesting her dance card, another suggested she join a party for the opera next week and Lord Jason Rutherford was coming to claim his dance.

He had been one of the first to scrawl his name on her dance card, and several times during the evening, Samantha had caught him staring at her. One of the other guests, a very pretty young girl, had also noticed his special attention, and remarked that Samantha should be flattered! "Rich as Croesus, you know. They say his estate in Sussex is enormous. And don't you think he's handsome?"

Well, yes, he was rather handsome, Samantha conceded now—tall and muscular, with sandy hair brushed forward Napoleon-style. He had sharp features, and, although his lips were thin, a rather charming smile. She returned his smile, taking his arm in a most natural way, as she excused herself to Desmond.

Desmond frowned as he watched them join the set. Although he had known Jason Rutherford all his life, he never thought of him as a friend. More like a friendly enemy. The competition had started on the rugby field when he was at Eton and Rutherford at Harrow, and had continued even after he left Oxford—this time at cards, racing, and women. He couldn't claim he disliked Rutherford. But...well, twice he had suspected him of cheating at cards, and he knew for sure that the man was a very poor loser. Still, he was a rather engaging chap and had a way with the women. Desmond did not like the way he was now smiling and talking in that animated fashion with Samantha.

Even more, Desmond had been irritated by Rutherford's significant nod to him as he led her away. Gad! Did the man regard Samantha as a prize trophy to be won in their continuing competition?

"My! How grim you look! I quite hesitate to approach you. And I was just going to compliment you on your mother's lovely ball!"

"Ball? Oh, yes . . . yes, indeed. Lovely." Coming out of his preoccupation, he forced himself to relax his tightened jaw, and tried to calm himself as he looked into the teasing face of a young lady. "And you are looking very lovely yourself," he added automatically as he slowly unclenched his fist.

CHAPTER EIGHT

DURING ONE of her morning visits, Lady Marlowe informed Samantha that an invitation to Lady Ashton's drum was almost equivalent to a card of admittance to Almack's. "Lady Ashton is one of the patronesses at Almack's, you know, and is a recognized leader of the ton. Everyone who is anyone will be there."

"Yes, indeed," agreed the duchess, "it will be a grand affair."

"As nice as the one you gave for us?" Emily asked.

"Oh, my dear, my intimate little gathering could not be compared to Lady Ashton's drum."

"Your grace, your party was delightful." Samantha would never have thought of it as an intimate gathering.

"Thank you, my dear, but it was nothing." Her grace's eyes held a provocative twinkle as she added, "Nothing at all compared to the kind of affair I could arrange should I have a special announcement to make."

Feeling a flush steal into her cheeks, Samantha bent her head and said nothing.

Her mind still on Lady Ashton's drum, Lady Marlowe frowned. "The eighteenth? Isn't that rather early?"

"Oh, Julia, she always sets it early," said the duchess. "A chance, she says, for the newcomers to get acquainted before the season gets into full swing."

"What newcomers?" The duke, who had not appeared to be listening, looked up from his book. "Only *old* families will be admitted to the Ashton's."

"Cedric!" his wife remonstrated.

He winked at Samantha. "New money, maybe. That is, if they don't smell too much of the shop."

"You're abominable!" The duchess flipped her lace handkerchief at him before using it to give her nose another of her nervous pats. "It will be one of the most delightful affairs of the season, and we will certainly not want to miss it."

Lady Marlowe asked the duke if he was following the diet she gave him. He said he was and that it seemed to be doing some good. He might even attend the Ashton drum himself.

So it was that, promptly at the fashionable hour of nine, the Duval party of six were among the fortunates who climbed the staircase to an elegant ballroom to be presented to Lord Henry Ashton and his lady, Elizabeth.

When they had made their greetings and moved a little away, Lord Desmond bent his head to catch Samantha's surprised whisper. "I didn't know there was a *Lord* Ashton."

His shoulders shook, but he kept his voice low as he answered. "Of course not. All you ever hear is Lady Ashton. She is the patroness. She gives the drum."

As if in confirmation, his mother's effusive exclamation was heard. "Lizzie, it is so beautiful. You've quite outdone yourself this time."

Their amused glances met and Lord Scarborough wanted to know what they were laughing at. "At the trials and tribulations of matrimony," Desmond answered. "Poor Henry Ashton. He had an identity of his own before he married."

"Ain't it true," agreed Lord Scarborough as he moved off to greet an old friend.

Desmond touched the hand resting lightly on his arm. "My little safeguard. I thank you for your protection, Samantha."

Samantha did not hear him. She was stunned by the magnificence before her. Never in all her life had she seen such a large ballroom in a private home. One wall consisted entirely of oval windows reaching from floor to ceiling. The potted palms between them were almost as tall as the windows. The opposite wall was lined with mirrors which repeated the whole scene and made the room seem even larger than it was. Scattered about were several gilded chairs with silk cushions woven in an intricate pattern of yellow and gold. Large golden urns held great sprays of yellow flowers. Footmen in gold uniforms served punch and champagne. Five chandeliers which must have held a hundred candles each hung from the ceiling and cast their golden glow on the moving throng. Gold-garbed musicians were gathered in an alcove at the end of the room, almost hidden by a bank of ferns.

Samantha felt the pressure of Desmond's hand on hers and looked up to see him smiling down at her. "Do you like it?"

"I—I think so."

"You're not sure?"

"It's just that I feel a little like Cinderella waiting for the clock to strike midnight."

He chuckled. "Don't worry, my dear. It's not midnight yet. First you must dance with the prince. Don't you remember?"

She raised one hand to her eyes and scanned the room. "Alas, kind sir, though I see many a gentleman in princely garb, I fear there is not a true prince among them. Or, is it that I don't recognize a prince when I see one?"

"Alas and alack for you, my poor nearsighted child. You may have to settle for a lowly marquis."

Samantha laughed and decided she was enjoying herself, though she was a bit overwhelmed by the grandeur.

Even Emily was subdued by the spectacle. She allowed herself to be led away by Arthur, who had evidently been watching for their arrival and had stumbled forward as soon as they appeared. He was resplendent in a lilac velvet coat and matching satin breeches, and they heard him murmur reprovingly as they moved away, "Emily, you're wearing blue! How could you!"

As the evening wore on, Samantha became more relaxed. As far as she could see, the Ashton ball went on much as other balls. Dance cards were requested, signed and returned; dance sets formed and dispelled as the music swelled and was silent; men smiled and bowed; fans fluttered flirtatiously; dowagers sat and gossiped; groups gathered and moved away, and there was a continuous congenial sound of talk and laughter.

In a pause between dances, Samantha found herself standing beside Lord Scarborough. He looked quite handsome in his amber-coloured evening coat, and she told him so. "It matches your eyes."

"Well, now, that's a nice compliment coming from a pretty chit like you. Turquoise. I told you that was a good colour for you. No, no, it ain't too low. And that old pendant of Agatha's really sets it off."

She touched the pendant. "Dear Aunt Agatha, she gave me all she had and this is the only piece I really like." Samantha wished her aunt could know how happily she was wearing it.

Lord Scarborough was looking anxiously around the hall.

"I haven't seen a card room," she told him.

"There ain't any," Desmond said as he joined them.

"No card room!" Lord Scarborough looked his dismay. "I never heard of such a thing."

Desmond shrugged. "Seems the lady likes her guests to mingle, not vanish to a card room."

"Well, if that don't beat all," Lord Scarborough moaned. "What's a fellow to do?"

"Mingle!" The word came simultaneously from Samantha and Desmond, and they both laughed at the expression on Lord Scarborough's face.

"Miss Scarborough, I believe this is our dance."

It was Lord Rutherford. Why, Samantha scolded herself as she took his hand, was she always so reluctant to move away from Desmond? She must get over this feeling! Learn to enjoy herself with other men. And Rutherford was most congenial—an excellent dancer and a good conversationalist, as interested in horses as she. She enjoyed the dance, smiled at his lavish compliments and skilfully evaded his too personal queries—the length of her planned stay in London, the duration and intimacy of her acquaintance with Desmond.

At the end of the set, the duchess claimed her attention. "Lord Rutherford, pray excuse us, I must present Samantha to Lord Shelton." She led Samantha to a man who was wearing a black velvet coat braided with gold. He was a little bent and held something in his ear.

"Lord Shelton, this is Samantha. Samantha Scarborough Agatha Weatherby's niece. WEATHERBY."

Now Samantha could discern that he was holding a hearing trumpet that evidently was not of much use, for the duchess had to shout to make herself heard. "WEATHERBY! No, her niece. SCARBOROUGH. You remember George Scarborough. No, no. He is deceased...deceased...DEAD. Yes, indeed. His brother. Over there."

Her grace directed Lord Shelton's attention to Stanley Scarborough, who was standing a little away conversing with two other gentlemen. "He's the one in the amber coat...amber.... Horses...yes, yes." She smiled, finding that Lord Shelton had finally caught the drift. "Scarborough...yes, quite famous. Very famous, indeed." Then she frowned defensively. "No, no, not a trader.... A hobby...HOBBY. He was interested in bloodlines...breeding. No, no...not reading. BREEDING. Did a great deal with bloodlines. Lord George Scarborough, you know. Yes. Lord.''

While the duchess talked and gesticulated, Samantha's attention was caught by a rather large woman in red who stood a little aside, intently listening to the conversation while appearing not to do so. Extending her hand to Lord Shelton, Samantha wondered vaguely who the woman was. Then she saw Jasper Marlowe approaching, and looked down at her card. Yes, this was his dance.

"Hello, Jasper." The duchess smiled at her nephew. "You know Lord Shelton, of course. Oh, there's Eliza Campbell. We must speak to her. You young people enjoy your dance.''

The young people could not do so immediately, for they were accosted by the lady in red. "Good evening, Mr. Marlowe, how do you do? And who is this pretty young lady? I don't believe we've met.''

"Good evening, Lady Atterley." Jasper's voice was stiff. "Miss Scarborough, this is Lady Atterley and her sister Miss—er—Miss Lindsey.''

For the first time Samantha noticed that there was another lady standing beside her. A young lady in yellow, her hair bound in a tight knot on top of her head.

Lady Atterley seized Samantha's hand. "I'm so glad to meet you, Miss Scarborough. Matilda's up for the season and I do want her to get to know some of the young people.'' She took Matilda's hand and placed it in Samantha's. "Now I'm going to give a party for her real soon, and I want you to come. I promise you it will be a gala affair.''

Samantha clasped the young woman's hand warmly. "Of course. My sister and I will be glad to come." She wished she could do something to comfort this embarrassed girl. *I know just how she feels,* Samantha thought, remembering her own first time in London.

"Please excuse us," said Jasper. "I believe the music has started."

"You go right ahead, you young stud." Lady Atterley poked Jasper with her fan and cast a significant glance toward his obviously pregnant Melissa, seated across the room with Lady Marlowe. "In a family way again? What is it now? Five—or six?"

"Four" was Jasper's curt answer as he pulled Samantha away.

"You shouldn't have hurried so," Samantha scolded. "Perhaps I could have secured a partner for Miss Lindsey. I know how it is to be the first time in London and—"

"It's not her first time. Lady Atterley's been trying for three seasons to get her off."

Poor thing. Three torturous seasons! Samantha, glancing back, saw Lady Atterley making her determined way toward Lord Scarborough, Matilda in tow.

Lord Scarborough looked up to see a large lady in red approaching him. Her face was familiar and he fumbled in his mind to put a name to it. Atterley. That was it. Peter Atterley's wife. He shut his eyes. Red. With that complexion she should never allow herself to be seen in anything other than grey or black.

"Lord Scarborough. How nice to see you again!"

He opened his eyes. "Good evening, Lady Atterley."

"I don't think you've ever met my sister. Matilda, darling, this is Lord Scarborough. Matilda Lindsey, Lord Scarborough."

He bent dutifully over the young lady's hand. "Miss Lindsey. Are you enjoying your...er...do you live in London?"

"No. She's visiting me for the season."

"Oh, how nice. Glad you could be here."

Miss Lindsey said nothing. Indeed she had no chance. For Lady Atterley rattled on. "I've been hearing such wonderful things about you and your horses, Lord Scarborough.''

"Horses?"

"Yes. And I want you to tell us all about them. All those marvellous things you do with them!"

"Do?" Whatever did he do besides bet on them?

"Oh, you are so modest! I've heard all about the Scarborough Stables!"

"Oh. Oh, yes, of course. The stables."

"So famous, you know. All that marvellous breeding."

"Breeding. Yes, yes. But I am afraid that was my brother, George. He—"

Lady Atterley's face fell. "I understood your brother was dead."

"Oh, yes, he is. Thing is…I meant…he started it. That is, I can't take the credit. And now it's all in Hawkins's hands."

"Hawkins? Another brother?"

"No. My—the trainer."

"Oh, yes. Indeed, indeed, indeed. Naturally you must have trainers. But, of course, you *own* the stables."

"Yes, I own them." Scarborough was getting tired of this exchange and sought to extricate himself. "Er, could I get you some refreshments?"

"Oh, how kind of you, Lord Scarborough! Of course you may take Matilda down to supper! Oh! There's Peter looking for me. Now you two just enjoy yourselves!"

Lord Scarborough watched Lady Atterley's hasty departure, wondering how he got into this and how he could get out.

"You don't have to."

"Eh?" He looked at the girl beside him. Yellow. Some people had no taste. Pity.

"You needn't take me down to supper." Her voice had a low throaty quality. Rather pleasing. Not loud and strident like her sister's. Gad, he was glad to see that woman go!

"It's no trouble at all. That is, I—"

"Please, sir. Don't apologize. I quite understand that was not your intention."

"Well, I . . . that is . . . er . . . good God! You ain't gonna cry, are you?" He took a quick look around. "Not the thing! Not here! It ain't . . . that is, it just ain't the thing!"

She blinked back the tears, but whispered ferociously, "I will not! No. I know she means it kindly. But I will not be forced upon you."

"There now, I ain't such a bad fellow. Upstanding. Gentleman—all that stuff."

That brought an unwilling smile to her lips. "It's not you. And I am persuaded you know that. It's me, and I don't think I can bear it another season!" The eyes were filling up again.

"Come now. This ain't the whole season. Just one night."

"You don't understand. It is a whole season. Lenora has me up and Mama makes me come. And I keep telling them it's no use, and they keep pushing and pushing."

The girl was definitely going to cry this time! He spoke sharply. "That's no face to present to a ballroom! Bad ton! Hold your head up and smile!"

She made an attempt. "I'm sorry. I'm behaving badly."

"No, no. Pretend it's brag."

"Brag?"

"Brag . . . pocher."

"Pocher?"

"A card game. And the fellow holding the best cards wins the game. Only sometimes you can fool him. See? Bluff! You put on a smug smile, a confident face, and he thinks you have the best cards and he throws his hand in, and you win. See?"

"I don't think so."

"That's what you have to do. Put on a good face."

"All right. I'll try." She did actually manage a smile. "Still, that's all right for you to say. You're a man. You can play cards or whatever you like. You don't have to be put on display and pushed at somebody. That's not fair."

"Quite right."

"People don't like you pushed at them."

"And goods should be properly displayed."

"Goods?"

"That dress. It don't suit."

She looked down at herself. "What's wrong with it?"

"Yellow. Washes you right out. Like a drowned... Don't suit."

"Oh, I'm sorry."

"Now don't go getting all upset. I didn't mean anything by it. Just that another colour would suit you better. You put your best foot forward, so to speak."

"Like that card game? Boast—no, brag."

"No. In brag you hide your best cards. On display, you have to enhance your best."

She sighed. "That is, if you have anything to enhance."

"Your eyes," he said. "Very fine. And very blue. You should wear blue."

She stared at him.

"And pull some of that hair down from the top of your head. You look like a spinster."

"I am a spinster."

"Don't have to look like one."

"Everything about me is spinsterish! Even my name. Matilda!"

"Change it."

"How do you change your name?"

"Easy. Let's see. Mattie? No. Tilly. How's that?"

She laughed, a laugh low and throaty like her voice. "You're a very funny man, Lord Scarborough."

"You're rather funny yourself, Tilly. Shall we go down to supper?"

She hesitated. "You really don't have to."

"I know. Miss Lindsey, may I have the honour of your company at supper?"

"I would be delighted," she said, and took his arm.

CHAPTER NINE

SEVERAL EVENINGS LATER the Duval party returned from Almack's rather early, as the duchess had complained of a headache. Lord Desmond surmised that the headache and early departure were a contrivance to get Emily out of the way of her most recent conquest, Lord Cecil Billington. He said nothing, however, escorted the ladies home and then accepted his mother's invitation to join them for refreshments. Ample time, he reflected, before he was to meet Angel.

He was surprised to find his father still up. Book and pipe in hand, the duke sat in his favourite chair by the fire. Probably waiting for him, Desmond thought, to charge him with an errand to his bankers or some such.

"Errand?" His father gave him a surprised look. "Oh, no. Not you. I was waiting for Samantha. Must get my revenge."

It was then that the marquis noticed the chessboard on the footstool. Lord Duval placed the chess pieces in order. "All right, young lady, we'll see who's champion tonight."

"Goodness, my lord! You'll wear the poor child out." His wife protested.

"Nonsense," said the duke.

"Well, do let her have her cup of tea."

"And what prevents one from drinking while playing chess?" The duke tossed a cushion to the floor. "There you are, Sam. You won't catch me with that queen ploy of yours tonight.''

"Do not insist, my lord.'' Her grace handed the duke his port and cast a meaningful look toward her son. "Perhaps Samantha would rather—that is, would not wish to play at this time.''

"Indeed I would, ma'am. I love it.'' Samantha smiled at the exasperated lady and gracefully seated herself on the cushion, spreading her skirt around her.

Lord Desmond caught his breath. He had thought green her best colour, but in that red velvet gown, with the firelight playing against it, Samantha's hair took on a vibrant glow of its own, and the pixie face that looked impishly up at his father was exquisitely alive—beautiful!

Yet the unfamiliar stirring in his breast had nothing to do with physical beauty. *She really is a delightful minx,* he thought, and his father's deep laugh confirmed the fact.

Yes, Samantha was amazingly different. So straightforward. None of that simpering, smirking cajolery he usually encountered. She had an open and frank way of speaking and her laughter was spontaneous and real. She was light and graceful on her feet, too. He enjoyed dancing with her. That is, when he got the chance—all that male competition. And there was that habit she had of attaching him to some forsaken female, as she had done at Almack's that very evening.

"Do you see that girl over there, my lord?''

"Mark,'' he had corrected.

"Oh, yes. Mark. Do you see her? The one in pink. It would quite make her evening, my lor—Mark, if you would stand up with her for just one dance.''

"You mean one dance with me would launch her?''

"Of course. Every gentleman in the room would seek her out to find what had attracted the most selective Lord Desmond's notice.''

His laughter rang out. "Do I detect a note of flattery, my love? Or possibly rebuke?"

"Neither. It's quite true." She looked frankly up at him. "You'll see. Try. Would you? Please, my—Mark."

The girl in pink was awkward, but gratifyingly grateful. And, true enough, she had not lacked for partners after his dance. Samantha had been right, and kind. She probably remembered her own first unsuccessful London season.

Well, there was nothing unsuccessful about this one. She seemed to be enjoying it immensely. Surprisingly, so was he. And he had expected it to be such a bore. He congratulated himself. A good scheme, this visit of hers. Never had he felt so much at ease.

Of course, his mother was now applying all her matchmaking tactics to wed him to Samantha. But that did not signify. They had made their own bargain, he and Samantha. He was safe.

Perhaps that was why he felt so comfortable with her. She was not angling for a wedding ring; nor was she, like Angel, expecting expensive trinkets. Samantha made no demands. Such a pleasure to attend a girl who wanted nothing in return.

He looked at Samantha, so completely absorbed in the chess game, and felt an unaccountable urge to show his gratitude. He would like to buy her some trinket—a diamond tiara like his mother's? It would look lovely in her hair.

"Isn't that so, Mark? Oh, how provoking! I believe you have not heard one word I've said."

"Your pardon, Mama," Desmond turned reluctantly.

"Lord Billington—I've just been telling Emily she should not be deceived by that very correct air of his."

Unable to circumvent the chess game, the duchess had taken up another concern—that of convincing the impressionable Emily that the fashionable and most elegant earl of Stanhope was not the gentleman he appeared. She was not succeeding.

Complacently munching on a biscuit, Emily widened her eyes in innocent surprise. "But, your grace, you introduced me to him—here, at your party. I thought he said he was your cousin."

Desmond suppressed a smile. That was a relationship her grace would like to deny.

"Well, yes," she admitted now, "but very distant. And, my dear, he is a bit of a rattle."

"A rattle?" Emily inquired.

"Mark, dear, do explain what I mean."

Desmond hesitated. Rattle? Billington was an unconscionable rake. But his mother would not wish him to tell Emily that. And certainly nothing of that scandal involving a certain lady of quality. "Lord Billington is sometimes very indiscreet," he said to Emily. "His behaviour is not always what it should be."

"Oh, but he is so agreeable," Emily protested. "He even quoted some pretty poetry. And he said I reminded him of a Grecian statue. Wasn't that quaint? Because of this hairstyle, you know." Emily tossed the long curl over her left shoulder.

"Oh, he can say some monstrous pretty things," the duchess declared. "But he says them first to one girl and then to another. One should never take him seriously."

"Oh?" Emily glanced with satisfaction at her reflection in the mirror above the mantel. "Perhaps he has just not found the girl to whom he is seriously attracted."

"It's not for lack of searching," Desmond muttered under his breath.

"His manner to me has been unexceptional," Emily said. "Am I forbidden to see him, ma'am?"

"Heavens, no!" was her grace's dubious answer.

Clever girl, Desmond thought. She knows the duchess would not ban her own cousin from the house. Too bad she did not also know how many dowagers with marriageable daughters had unsuccessfully set their caps for that same title—and how many, after a certain unmentionable event, now steered their susceptible daughters away from such an unscrupulous charmer.

"Oh, I am so glad," said Emily, "for he has promised to take me to see the wax museum, and I wouldn't miss that for the world!"

"But, child," persisted her grace, "there are so many more eligible suitors. That young man—Traylor?"

"Travis, Arthur Travis. Just a childhood friend," Emily said, dismissing him with a shrug. "Lord Billington's an earl, isn't he?"

"Yes," Desmond answered. *A rake, a scoundrel, a philanderer!* he thought, but "Yes," he said to Emily, "he's an earl."

Looking as if that quite settled the matter, Emily glanced again at the mirror and meticulously adjusted a curl.

Desmond had been watching the chess game during this interchange and now gave it his full attention. "Wait, don't make that move," he said to Samantha. "You're much too free with your queen."

The duke waved him away. "You keep out of it. I think I've got her this time. I've finally caught on." Evidently he had not, for a few minutes later his king was hopelessly entrapped. "All right, you win," he conceded. "One for you, one for me. We'll have one more—best two out of three."

"No, Cedric, no more tonight. Time to retire."

Though reluctant, his grace arose immediately, responding as he always did when a sharp "Cedric" replaced his lady's usual more conciliatory "your grace."

Emily declared that she was tired, as she had danced every dance, and must be up early to go visit the wax museum in the morning.

The door shut behind the three and Desmond chuckled as he turned to Samantha. "Finally my mother's purpose has been achieved. The two lovers are alone at last."

Samantha looked up, a worried frown on her brow. "Oh, Mark, do you think it right to tease her so?"

Mark! At last his name came easily to her lips. It gave him a good feeling.

"She is so kind," Samantha continued, "I think we are taking advantage—"

"Enough of that! You are the best thing that has happened to this house for months. An excellent excuse for Mama to attend all the balls. And my father! I've never seen him so happy. Did you notice he never mentioned his leg?"

"He gets so absorbed in the game." Samantha smiled and began to put away the chess pieces.

"Hold on there! Just set the pieces in place. I think I'll have a go at this game. Do you know your method of play is most unorthodox?"

Samantha gave a quick glance at the clock. Gad! Did she think he had a timepeeper? "Come, come! You take the white and give me the black." He sat in his father's chair and began to set up the board.

"Ah!" he said a few minutes later. "Out you go with that queen first thing. Don't you know that's your most valuable piece?"

"Surely you mean the king," she said demurely.

"Imp! You know what I mean. The queen should always be protected because she has the greatest freedom of movement."

"Which is exactly why she should be used." Samantha made her next move and sighed. "That's just like a man. He never realizes the full value of a woman because he's so busy protecting her."

"Careful, my love! You sound much like a bluestocking!" Desmond brought out his rook, readying it for the attack.

Samantha laughed. "Oh, no, my lord. I'm no bluestocking, but I do believe our world would be in much better order if the women in it had just one half the freedom of this little lady." She picked up her queen and placed it directly in front of his king. "Checkmate," she said quietly.

Desmond stared in stupefaction. Damnation! She had checked his king in less than seven moves. "Set them up again," he said. "I'll have to watch that queen."

He did watch, capturing her queen early in the game. The second game lasted much longer. Twice he thought he had her, but in the end she checked him with one rook and a knight.

He laughed good-naturedly. "You're a tricky little one, you know! You jump that knight as easily as you take Sheba over a hedge."

He saw her face cloud and spoke softly. "You miss the rides with Sheba?"

"Oh, yes," she said, then added quickly, "but of course I enjoy the rides in the park."

"But much too tame compared to a gallop across the moor?"

"Well, yes." She laughed. "But that does not signify. We will soon be home."

Now why did that make him feel a little sad? "Tell you what. I'm taking you to Ascot tomorrow. Would you like that?"

She turned a radiant face toward him, and he could not keep the surprise any longer. "Hawkins has entered Black Knight. You'll see him race tomorrow."

"Oh, Mark, how wonderful!" She touched his arm. "This is your doing. I know you suggested it. Thank you, thank you."

Quite mesmerized, he watched the sparkle in the green eyes, the deepening of the dimple, the full delicate curve of the lips against even white teeth. What would it be like to kiss those lips?

With admirable restraint, he allowed his thumb to gently stroke her hand, still resting on his arm. The remarkable softness compelled him to turn her palm upward and press his lips into the sweetness. The touch of her hand was more thrilling than any other woman's lips.

There was a moment's hesitation and Samantha gently withdrew her hand, but not before Desmond caught the faint flush in her cheek—and a startled yet responsive gaze in her eyes. She turned quickly, embarrassed.

"It's late," he said when he could find his voice. "I must be off and you must go to bed." In silence he led her toward the stairs, watched her ascend, then let himself out.

"Where to, my lord?" Clinton asked as Desmond climbed into the waiting carriage. The marquis stared blankly at his groom.

Clinton had taken up the step, but was still holding the carriage door. "Well, sir, it's late. The theatre's closed."

He had forgotten Angel! There'd be the devil to pay tomorrow. But tonight... He yawned sleepily. "My own quarters, of course, Clinton."

CHAPTER TEN

SAMANTHA WATCHED in astonishment as Lord Desmond manoeuvred his tilbury through the vast number of vehicles crowding the streets of Berkshire. Were they all going to Ascot?

"Yes," said Desmond, carefully guiding his horses around a loaded stagecoach. At least six people were packed, inside with fifteen men on top.

Samantha was amazed at the variety of conveyances, as well as the assortment of occupants. Lords and ladies in phaetons, tilburys, barouches and carriages, dandies in hackney cabs, farmers with wives and daughters in wagons, an old stagecoach loaded with Oxford scholars. All were laughing and joking, in the gayest of moods.

"It will be a crush," said Samantha as one coachman blew his two-foot horn and swerved past them. "Will they all get to see the race?"

"Good God, no," Desmond said with a laugh. "Half just come to see the crowd, anyway." He nodded toward a group with a picnic basket, settling themselves along the side of the road. "They will enjoy their sandwiches and ale while watching the royal procession. They won't see one race, but they will enjoy a holiday."

Samantha, too, felt in a holiday mood. Her excitement mounted as Desmond drew up to the entry, helped her alight and tossed a guinea to an attendant who led the horses away.

They were admitted to the enclosed track through a turnstile. Samantha stared across the track at a tiered grandstand which appeared to be packed with people, all in different modes of dress, some even in masquerade. They were all standing and were packed together like sausages. And still more were coming. It was a squeeze, Samantha thought, and wondered if she was overdressed in her smart pink muslin and the wide pink hat trimmed with large silk flowers of deep rose.

But when Desmond led her toward another grandstand, she was glad that the duchess had insisted she wear that outfit. For here all the ladies were elegantly clad; all wore big wide hats with elaborate trimming. The men, she noted, were all dressed as Desmond—white trousers, black jacket, black top hats. Correct attire, she presumed, for a gentleman attending the Ascot races.

In this grandstand the people were comfortably seated, each group of friends in their own box. Attendants scurried around, serving champagne and ices to the ladies, brandy and cigars to the men. No squeeze here. They were as comfortable as in an opera house.

Already seated in the neighbouring box were Lord and Lady Atterley, and her sister, Miss Lindsey, whom Samantha had met at Lady Ashton's ball. Today Lady Atterley was wearing purple. Her hat was straw and was elaborately trimmed with red and purple flowers fashioned in velvet. The hat tilted to one side, whether by design or pulled over by the weight of the flowers one could not tell, but it gave her a rather rakish appearance. Miss Lindsey was garbed in blue, and Samantha thought she did not look quite as drab as she had seemed at the ball.

Shortly after their arrival, Desmond and Lord Atterley excused themselves to go down and discuss their bets with Lord Scarborough.

"Here, come over and sit beside me, dear," Lady Atterley invited Samantha, "and we will have a cosy chat."

Scanning the list of entries given her by Desmond, Samantha turned to her, ready to discuss the relative merits of each horse.

But Lady Atterley's mind was in another direction. "Your uncle," she said, speaking almost as if to herself, "is a fine figure of a man."

Samantha followed her gaze to Lord Scarborough, who was bent over a racing form with Lord Desmond. "Yes," she answered absently, "I suppose he is."

"Yes, indeed. A fine figure of a man. Nor purse pincher, either, I can tell."

"No. He's not." Certainly no one could call Uncle Stanley a purse pincher.

"Now I tell you plain, Miss Scarborough, if there's anything I can't abide, it's a clutch-fisted man. Take my Peter now. Openhanded as I always knew he would be. Don't stint on my pin money or anything else I want. A good man, I tell you."

"You are indeed fortunate."

"You are fortunate, too, you and your sister. You're his wards, ain't you?"

"His . . . Oh, you mean Uncle Stanley. Yes, we are his wards."

"And he's generous? I mean, good to you?"

"Oh, yes. Very kind."

Lady Atterley nodded. "I knew it! One look at you and I could tell. It's like I told Lady Ashton. That gown—the one you wore the other night, and that blue one with all that beadwork that your sister had on. One look was all I needed to know that you were attired by the finest modiste in London."

"Thank you." Samantha stirred restlessly, but Lady Atterley seemed not to notice.

"Yes, indeed, if I know anything, I do know quality when I see it." She smoothed the folds of her dress. "I can read it like a book. Quality in clothes. And quality in a man.'' Her gaze again drifted toward the men. "Yes, indeed. A fine figure of a man. I'm glad I brought Matilda.''

"Oh, do you like the races?'' Samantha, anxious to include Miss Lindsey in the conversation, leaned across to speak to her.

But Lady Atterley answered for her. "Good gracious, no! Matilda don't seem to enjoy anything, except maybe a book. And that's what I can't understand. I ain't much for reading myself. I tell her, you ain't going to meet anyone in a book!''

"True.'' Samantha refrained from adding that was hardly the purpose of reading a book.

"But my little sister is so shy.'' The lady gave Matilda's hand a pat. "It's so difficult for her to meet people. That's why I would like her to get to know you better.''

"That would be nice.''

"I'm going to send you an invitation to the gala I am planning for her birthday.''

"That would be nice,'' Samantha repeated.

"Except that I have been thinking maybe I should give a small dinner party first. Matilda's not one to push herself forward, you know. But if she had a few intimate friends around her, then she would feel more comfortable at a big affair.''

"That would make it easier.''

"Then you would come? To a small dinner party, I mean. You and your sister?'' Her eyes were almost pleading.

"Of course I will come.''

"Oh, thank you! Let's see—your sister, and who is that young man who was with her? And Lord Desmond. And, of course, your uncle. I will send cards.'' The matter of the dinner party seemed to give Lady Atterley a deal of satisfaction. She leaned comfortably back and smiled, murmuring almost inaudibly, "Yes, indeed. A fine figure of a man."

Turning to her list, Samantha was again diverted by Lady Atterley, whose attention was now on other people.

"See that lady passing our box," she began, and launched into long discussion about who was who, who had married whom and which high-in-the-instep duchess had tried to snub her. "And Lord, such a set-down as Peter gave her."

A detailed version followed, but Samantha hardly heard. Her attention was on a woman of exquisite beauty who was entering the box on the other side. A raven-haired woman with dark, deep-set eyes, finely arched eyebrows, lily-white skin and lips too rosy to be real. Her wide white hat did not conceal, but cleverly exposed, the silky black hair arranged in a loose coil on the back of her neck. The pure white of the hat and the gown contrasted vividly with the dark hair and stood out against the black jacket of the bearded gentleman who escorted her. Just before she took her seat, she glanced toward Desmond. His eyebrow went up and he smiled almost mockingly. The lady's answering nod was cool, but her eyes flashed with feeling.

There had been something decidedly intimate in the exchange, Samantha thought. Who was she?

"A nobody!" came Lady Atterley's low voice, as if Samantha had asked the question aloud. "Don't look at her, Samantha. All right if I call you 'Samantha'? I ain't too much for formality, you know. Turn this way. Nothing but a common actress. Angel D'Angelo, she calls herself, and Lord knows what her real name is. Born in a workhouse, they say. Made it this far on her face and figure."

That was not surprising, Samantha thought, noting how the soft material of the woman's dress clung, audaciously outlining each curve of the beautifully rounded figure.

Lenora Atterley gave a sniff. "Aiming for a title, she is. That's Lord Chesterfield with her now, and he ain't the only one. Men are such fools. But they'd better be careful about this one. She might look like a lady, but you can't make a tulip out of a tart, I always say. Oh, my! Here he comes. Everything will start now!''

The men returned to their boxes, everyone stood and there was a great fanfare as the royal procession began. When the King's party was seated in the royal box, the trumpets stopped, and an excited lull preceded the start of the races.

Samantha returned to her seat beside Desmond, and Lady Atterley somehow manoeuvred so that Miss Lindsey sat closest to the Desmond party, nearest to Lord Stanley. As the horses for the first race passed in review, her uncle tapped Samantha on the shoulder. ''All right, Sam. I'm relying on you. Where shall I place my bet?''

''Timerlake,'' Samantha answered without hesitation.

''He's a rather scrawny little thing,'' Desmond observed.

''Scrawny, but sturdy,'' she said. ''Foaled out of Sunset by Blue Ribbon, an excellent combination. He will do well against this group.''

''If you're that sure,'' Stanley declared, ''I'll put a hundred pounds on him.''

''One hundred pounds? Oh, Lord Scarborough. Surely—'' Miss Lindsey broke off in sudden confusion. She had hardly uttered a word before this, and Lord Scarborough stared at her in some surprise.

''You think I should lay more on him?'' he asked?

''More! Oh, no! What I meant was—''

''What she meant was that maybe Flightwood would be the better risk,'' Lady Atterley broke in. ''Grey, you see. I always say, a grey horse is a lucky horse.''

Lord Scarborough looked hard at Lady Atterley, then turned back to her sister. ''Is that what you meant to say?''

"Well, I should hope she ain't trying to advise you," Lady Atterley chortled. "Why this is the first race she's ever attended. She don't know one horse from another."

Lord Scarborough bristled. Drat the woman! Don't ever permit a person to have his say. And this poor child hardly had a chance. He turned his back on Lady Atterley and again spoke to Matilda. "Well, now, what was it you did mean to say?"

"Well, I thought . . . That is . . ." She fumbled with her reticule. "It's . . . well, it's an awful lot of money. To chance it all on one horse."

"But that's what one does at a race, don't you see? At the races—each time, I mean, you place your bet on one horse. Nothing ventured, nothing gained."

"But to risk such an enormous sum!"

"Now don't be in such a quake. It ain't much of a risk when Sam does the picking." Stanley laughed as he went off to post his bet.

It was Samantha who heard Lady Atterley's whispered admonition to her sister. "Lord, Matilda! Don't be such a ninny. The gentry always play high. Why, you can tell a gentleman by the amount of his wager as well as by the cut of his coat!"

Thus reprimanded, the poor girl lapsed again into silence, and, beyond telling Lord Scarborough she was prodigiously happy for him every time he won, she uttered not another word during the entire day.

Relying on Samantha's judgement, Uncle Stanley had quite a few winners. When she had successfully picked three horses for him, the other men began to trust her judgement, also. Often she was not sure, and said so. But always she knew the lineage and the breeder, and, more often than not, the winner. The men were jubilant as they went to the betting stand to collect their winnings and confidently to place their bets.

There was another fanfare before the running of Ascot's most important Gold Cup race. Desmond, who had attended the Jockey Club dinner given by the King two weeks before, was certain that the King's horse would win. The King, he declared, had bought seven horses for which he paid a monstrous sum, with Spendthrift the top of the lot. "The King has never won the Gold Cup, you know, and he is determined to have it this year."

"I fear he will be disappointed," said Samantha as she scanned her list.

"Oh?" Desmond queried.

"Unless he bought Zingaree," Samantha continued. "I think he will be the winner."

Desmond's eyes quickened with interest. "No," he said. "Zingaree was offered to the King, but he refused him. He was bought just two hours ago by Lord Chesterfield here. Chesterfield—" he turned to the bearded man in the next box "—you did buy Zingaree, didn't you?"

For answer, Chesterfield pointed to the horses now parading for review.

"Yes," said Desmond. "He is carrying the Chesterfield colours. Shall we place our bets, gentlemen?"

When Zingaree bounded first across the finish line, the disappointed King departed with his company. But the men who had followed Samantha's advice happily collected their winnings. Samantha did not bet, but was enjoying herself immensely. She felt on familiar ground with these horses, many of whom had been bred by her father. How she loved a race.

But now. Now was the best part. Black Knight was in the next race. Tears came into her eyes as she watched the princely black stallion, mounted by Hawkins's eldest boy, Tab, wearing the Scarborough colours.

"He will win this race by at least three lengths," she declared. "And one day here, he will win the Gold Cup and the Classic at Newmarket."

Her heart gave a great leap as, true to her word, Black Knight crossed the finish line four lengths ahead of the others. In honour of the win, Desmond ordered champagne all around. Samantha raised the glass to her lips as he made the toast "To a fine horse, and to the lovely lady who owns him." It was the highlight of one of the happiest days she had spent in London.

Just before they departed, the beautiful lady in white left her box and walked in front of them on the arm of Lord Chesterfield, and again Samantha was struck by her grace and beauty. Lady Atterley had said she was "a common actress." She must be a very accomplished one, Samantha thought, and in spite of Lady Atterley's unfaltering comments, she could not help but feel a certain respect for someone who had been born in a workhouse and now carried herself with such grace and dignity. She also noted the way Lord Desmond's gaze followed the couple, and a vague apprehension tinged with sadness nudged her. But she pushed it aside. This had been an enjoyable day, she had seen Black Knight win, and Lord Desmond's interests were of no concern to her!

As they settled themselves into his curricle, Lord Rutherford rushed up. "Do hold a minute, Desmond," he begged. "I want to thank Miss Scarborough. She has done me the greatest favour."

"Oh?" Desmond politely checked his horses, though he was anxious to leave. He did not like the way Rutherford was looking at Samantha.

"What favour?" she asked, smiling but puzzled.

"Timberlake. You told me to buy him. And he won the very first race today. Don't you remember?"

"Oh, yes, that's right. How lucky for you. But I certainly did not tell you to buy him."

"But you talked about him and his bloodlines that day at the ball. You told me all about him. And I went out and made the purchase the very next day. Thank you, Miss Scarborough.''

"Well, I am happy for you," she said with a laugh. "But I can certainly take no credit."

"Indeed you must. And I want to show you my Miss Silver. Remember—"

"Sorry, Rutherford. It's rather congested here, and I must be off. Goodbye." Desmond flicked the reins and the horse quickly pulled away.

Samantha looked at him. "Oh, Mark. You didn't give him time to finish what he was going to say."

"I had to pull out when I could."

"But you hardly spoke to him. You were quite rude. Don't you like him?"

He shrugged. "Let's just say he is not a favourite among my acquaintances. And really, Sam, I cannot approve of your being so intimate with him."

"Intimate! Heavens, I've hardly spoken to the man except to talk of horses."

"To the extent of advising which horse he should buy," he snapped.

"I certainly did not!"

"Of course you didn't." Desmond was immediately vexed with himself. His dislike of Rutherford was only instinctive. And he had no valid reason to discredit him to Samantha. "I—I'd just rather you didn't see too much of him. But I shouldn't have spoken as I did. I'm sorry. Forgive me?"

"Well, I don't know whether I shall forgive you or not. And I cannot see why you would not wish me to see him. He's quite affable. And the gossip among my female friends is that—let's see…what have I heard. Oh, yes, he's an earl, for he came into his inheritance early, you know. An only son—greatly indulged by a doting mother. Extremely wealthy with an extensive estate at Sussex." She dimpled as she gave Desmond a mischievous glance.

"Your speaking ill of him seems rather like the pot calling the kettle black."

"I did not speak ill of him!" Desmond said, resenting the comparison. But he could not help adding, "And I am certainly not a poor loser!"

"Oh, a poor loser, is he? Well, I think that is rather to his credit. I think I'll ask him to speak with Uncle Stanley, who is much too good-natured about losing. If he became a *poor* loser he might not gamble so much." She laughed, then looked thoughtfully up at him and touched his arm. "My goodness gracious! Don't get into such a pucker. I was only funning. And indeed, that's quite enough of Lord Rutherford. Oh, Mark, wasn't it thrilling to see Black Knight cross the finish line?"

CHAPTER ELEVEN

A FEW DAYS LATER cards arrived inviting Emily and Samantha to dine at the home of Lord and Lady Peter Atterley.

"Oh, dear," said the duchess when she was consulted. "She has scheduled it very carefully when there are no other assemblies."

"But that is good, isn't it?" Samantha was rather puzzled. "That means we can accept."

Her grace sighed. "I don't see how you can refuse."

"Well, then, I'll just write a note of acceptance now, as I can see you are not quite ready to leave." She wrote the note and sent it off by a groom before joining her hostess for their proposed visit to Hookham's library.

At Hookham's they encountered Lady Marlowe, who suggested they join her for tea at Bonwit's. They had not been seated very long in the elegant tearoom, when the subject of the Atterley invitation was broached. The duchess mentioned it in what appeared to Samantha to be an overly casual manner.

There was nothing casual about the way the news was received by Lady Marlowe. "Really, Sylvia, you should not permit the girls to become intimate with that upstart."

The duchess remarked almost apologetically that they could hardly refuse an invitation to Lord Atterley's. "Why, we have known him for—oh, my goodness, how many years!" She nervously peeled off her gloves. "Anyway, Julia, one dinner engagement could hardly be the basis for an intimate friendship.''

"You think not!'' Lady Marlowe set her cup down with a clatter. "Just you wait until Lenora Atterley goes quacking about her intimate friend Samantha Scarborough. No, let's see...Matilda's dearest friend—they're so inseparable, you know. That's just how she'll put it.''

"Now, Julia.''

"You know how she latches on to people, Sylvia.''

"Oh, yes, but I hardly think...''

"She's been trying for years to push Matilda onto somebody. And she's always trying to form intimate friendships with any girl likely to attract men. It's the only way she can get Matilda to meet them. Heaven knows that fubsy-faced girl can't attract anyone herself.''

"Really, Julia, you make too much of this.''

"And Mark is going?'' Lady Julia gave her sister a knowing look. "I would not be at all surprised if Lenora Atterley was not right now planning to have Matilda throw her cap at Mark.''

The duchess's mouth curved in smug satisfaction. "That may be. I am sure there are many ladies ready to toss their cap in his direction. But I think we need have no fear for Mark. Not anymore.''

Samantha bit into a sweetmeat and tried to avoid the sly look the duchess sent in her direction.

"Well, you just can't be too careful.'' Lady Marlowe poured herself another cup of tea. "Two years ago, you know, she tried to form an intimacy with Melissa. She kept dropping by, leaving her card and inviting Melissa to tea. But Jasper put his foot down and scotched that in the bud.''

"How?'' Her grace looked as if she really wanted to know.

"Melissa was expecting—which child?'' Lady Julia's face took on a pensive look. "Percy? No, I believe it was·

Priscilla. Jasper said right off that his wife was in a delicate condition and it was no time for her to be gadding about in society."

"Well, I am afraid we don't have that excuse. And I am afraid the duke would never forgive me if I offended Lord Atterley."

"I suppose not. It is a shame." Lady Julia shook her head. "How that common Lenora Lindsey ever got to be Lady Atterley is beyond me. He was practically betrothed to Louise Littleton, you know."

"Yes, I know. And I know that she is one of your dearest friends. But this is water under the bridge now, Julia. Samantha, dear, I am afraid you will have to go."

"Oh, of course," said Samantha. "I really don't mind. And I did promise Lady Atterley."

"Just don't get too intimate with her. A mushroom."

"She—she seems quite friendly," Samantha ventured.

"Too friendly. Common, you know. And you can't make a silk purse out of a sow's ear. Peter Atterley's mother would turn over in her grave if she knew who was mistress of her house now."

Samantha kept her thoughts to herself, but she pitied Matilda more than ever. Not only to be presented awkwardly through three London seasons, but to be presented in the company of a sister who was so reluctantly admitted to the ton. She resolved to do all in her power to make the poor girl feel more at ease.

So she was firm with Lord Scarborough. "No, Uncle, indeed, you cannot cry off."

"Dash it all, I would like to know why not. You will be with Desmond and Emily will have young Travis. What do you need with me?"

"You are a man."

"Damme, Sam, I know I'm a man. What has that to do with anything?"

"It has to do with balance."

"Balance?" Lord Stanley's irritation showed in his face.

"You know very well that men and women must be balanced for a proper dinner party. You are a single man, and that means she must have invited some single female guest."

"Plenty of macaronis around just dying to go to the parties."

Not to this one, Samantha thought, but did not say so. "Perhaps they are not known to Lady Atterley. Anyway, it's too late to procure a man to take your place. It would be excessively rude to cry off, Uncle. You must know that."

Lord Stanley relented, but not in his usual good spirits. "All right, Sam. But I tell you plain, I'll be devilish glad when this season is over. All this balancing and escorting don't leave a man time to attend to his own affairs. Just as the gaming gets going at White's, I'll be toddling off to some dashed dinner party."

Emily was always eager to attend any party, but did she have to go with Arthur? Lord Billington had more dash.

"He may have dash," agreed Samantha, "but what he does not have is a card to Lady Atterley's dinner party. Arthur has. I'm afraid you have no choice."

Lord Desmond made no protestations. Anticipating his objections, Sam had told him that she particularly wanted to go, and hoped he would not think a small dinner party too dull.

"Dull?" His gaze was enigmatic. "An evening spent in your company? Never!"

Her heart gave a little flutter, but she suppressed her excitement, saying only that she was glad he did not object. She would hate to disappoint Matilda.

It was good that she had prevailed upon them all to go, for, to her surprise, they were the only guests. They were shown by the butler into an elegantly furnished, rather oversize drawing room, and their hosts rose to greet them.

Lord Scarborough shut his eyes.

"Don't, Uncle. Bad ton," Samantha whispered mischievously.

He opened his eyes and tried to erase the pained expression from his face.

Samantha could hardly blame him. The satin sheen of Lady Atterley's dress emphasized the bright red so unbecoming to her ruddy complexion, and the fullness of the skirt gave her the appearance of a floating balloon descending upon them.

She greeted them effusively. "Samantha, how sweet of you to come. And you look positively divine. I just love bright colours, don't you? And Emily—it is Emily, ain't it? I told your sister, I ain't one to be formal. Lord Desmond. Mr. Travis."

She stopped for a moment, staring at Arthur's brocaded puce coat with wide padded shoulders, a flowered weskit, and satin breeches tied at the knees with those strings he fancied. "A regular tulip, ain't you?" Lady Atterley poked Arthur with her fan.

But it was Lord Scarborough whose hand she clasped so warmly and upon whom she fastened a fond gaze. "Lord Scarborough," she cooed. "I am so glad you could be with us this evening. I know how busy you are. Always careering about the country with your horses."

He blinked. "Careering about with my...? Oh. Oh, yes. I had planned to post down to Doncaster, but—" He caught Samantha's warning glance and faltered. "Well, that is, glad to be here," he finished lamely.

Lady Atterley, who had hardly heeded his words, called to her sister, who was hovering quietly in the background. "Matilda, dearest, do come here and greet your guests." She placed Miss Lindsey's hand in Lord Stanley's as if bestowing upon him a priceless gift. "I know you are acquainted with Matilda. You were so taken with her at the Ashton's drum. I had to warn her it ain't proper for a lady.

to dance more than two sets with the same gentleman. Have to be careful with our young beauties, you know."

Miss Lindsey hastily withdrew her hand and spoke quietly, turning her head to include all of them in her greeting. "We are so glad to have you."

Samantha moved quickly forward. "It is so good to see you again, Miss Lindsey. So kind of Lord and Lady Atterley to invite us."

Matilda led Samantha to a sofa across the room and sat down beside her.

"A lovely evening," said Samantha.

"Yes," said Matilda.

"Are you—well, that is . . ." Samantha decided not to ask if she was enjoying her London visit. "I hope we will be good friends."

"I hope so, too. My sister says . . . That is, I have so few friends in London."

Why, thought Samantha, her eyes are quite beautiful. Almost as blue as Emily's. She had not noticed before. It must be the dress. Blue, and in the latest mode. Her hair was not so fashionably curled, but at least it was no longer in that horrible topknot.

"You look quite fetching," Samantha told her. "I like that dress."

An unfortunate remark, for it was caught by Lady Atterley and allowed her again to focus attention on Matilda. "Ain't it elegant? And just think, Matilda made it herself." She made this announcement to the entire room. "Matilda is very clever. Makes her own clothes. We spent all day Monday at the linen merchant's and she selected several lengths—silks, muslins and what have you. Thing was, she had to have them all in blue. I told her that would get powerful monotonous. But, no, she must have only blue. Matilda, get up and let Lord Desmond have that seat by Samantha. You sit here, next to Lord Scarborough. Now, Peter, you stop gaping at Miss Emily. I know she's a pretty young thing, but you let Mr. Travis have that chair and you come over here and sit by me. Now we are in balance, ain't we? One thing I can't abide is for all the women to be bunched together, cackling to one another.'' She pulled on a bell rope and a footman appeared with a tray of canapés.

It would not be quite correct to say that conversation flowed that evening as they sat munching canapés and sipping sherry and ratafia, but it limped along as each guest spoke to his designated partner.

Arthur told Emily that it looked as though it were going to be a devilish dull evening and he'd just as soon they were somewhere else, except that almost anywhere else that blasted Lord Billington would be dancing attendance on her.

Emily inspected her small satin slippers and reflected that at least they would be dancing, and that would certainly be better than this.

Lord Scarborough looked at the silent girl beside him and remarked that yes, the blue did credit to her eyes.

''Thank you,'' she said, and looked down at her folded hands.

Poor little thing, he thought. ''Shouldn't look so bored, you know. Bad ton.''

''Oh, I'm sorry. I'm not bored.''

''Then don't look like it. Remember what I told you about that game—brag. Put on a good face.''

She tried to smile. ''I forgot. I'm sorry.''

''Being pushed again?''

''Yes.''

''At me again, eh?''

''Yes. I'm sorry.''

''That don't signify. Ain't we friends?''

''Oh, yes.'' Relief was in her voice.

''Then just be friendly. Let's see . . . you can start out by asking how I did at Ascot the other day.''

She almost giggled. "I know how you did at Ascot. And I told you that I was prodigiously happy for you."

"So you did. So you did. And looked immensely relieved." He laughed. "I take it you don't approve."

"Oh, I wouldn't presume to disapprove!" She frowned. "It's just that—well, I am so much in the habit of economizing. But, of course, a gentleman has the right to decide on the amount of his wager."

"And a lady, my dear, has the right to express her opinion. Don't let anyone tie up your tongue." He gave her hand a little pat.

She smiled at him. "I am glad you did so well at Ascot."

"Yes, indeed. A very good day. Now let's see, I'll ask you . . ." He studied her. "Let's see, what will I ask you?"

"What have I read recently?" she suggested.

"Oh. Bookish, are you?"

"Yes." She sighed. "I suppose I am. And that's just what Lenora tells me I shouldn't be."

"Ah. Pushing again, eh?"

"Well, no. Pulling me away, more likely."

"Pushing. Pulling. All the same. Shouldn't allow it."

She stared at him, but said nothing.

"You should do what you want for a change."

"You really believe that?"

"I do, indeed," said Lord Scarborough, and wondered why he was not at this moment at White's, playing faro.

Desmond remarked to Samantha that he might have overstated the fact when he said an evening spent with her could never be dull.

"Wretch!" Samantha laughed. "What an impolite thing to say when I'm trying so hard to be pleasing and charming."

"An evening like this sorely tests even your charms."

"You're abominable. Try exerting some charm of your own."

He smiled and said that at least it would be interesting watching Stanley avoid the trap.

"What trap?"

"The one that's being set for him, with Matilda as the bait."

Samantha looked across the room at Miss Lindsey. "That shy girl? She couldn't toss her cap at anyone."

"Not she. Her sister's doing the tossing."

Samantha watched Lady Atterley's smiling animated face. Indeed she was a managing sort of woman! And she had made such a point of presenting Matilda to Uncle Stanley. Had she herself done wrong in persuading him to come—to be the extra man? For Matilda?

Then she shrugged, brightening. "Nonsense," she told Desmond. "Uncle Stanley has been a bachelor for a long time. And I daresay this is not the first time a cap has been tossed at him. He knows how to go on."

"I do hope so, for his sake."

"You needn't look so smug. It may be you she has her eye on. Indeed, your Aunt Julia seems to think so."

"You forget, my love. I am yours. I am quite safe." He took her hand and held it tenderly.

Samantha tapped him playfully with her fan. "Only for the season. Then I shall cast you adrift in a sea of tossing caps! Beware!"

"And yet will I survive," he promised, his shoulders shaking.

A plain man but with a pleasant enough countenance, Lord Peter Atterley, looked anxiously at his guests and suggested to his lady that they might set up card tables after dinner.

"Indeed we will not," she told him, and turned to the visitors. "Peter's talking about playing cards after dinner. Now a thing I can't abide is folks sitting pushing cards around when they could be having an interesting conversation. No, indeed, Peter, we plan to enjoy ourselves this evening."

Lord Peter sat silent for a few moments. Then, as if deciding that since conversation was the order of the day he should converse, he leaned across Lady Atterley and pleasantly asked Lord Scarborough if he had ever attended the Salisbury Agricultural Show.

Lord Scarborough, who knew nothing of agricultural shows except that they were good places to stay away from, said he had not had that pleasure.

Lord Atterley said he should make it a point to attend this year. "Always held in the fall, you know." Lord Atterley spoke with pride. "I may say that the Atterley estate has a pretty good record. For the past ten years we have been first in the pig contest and last year we took the blue ribbon for our turnips."

"Never mind about that, Peter," admonished Lady Atterley. "Ain't he a card? Hard enough to get him away from the country, and when he is away he prattles about pigs and turnips and such. If I didn't make him come up for the season, he'd be out everyday, worrying his tenants about what they were feeding their pigs."

She turned to Samantha. "Did you, Miss Scarborough, see that new play at the Apollo?"

Lord Atterley fell silent as his wife rattled on about the play. When a footman had served hot consomé to the guests and retreated, Lord Atterley looked at the tiny cup in his hand and groaned. "Hardly a swallow. Newfangled idea of Lenora's—got it in France—to serve the first course in the drawing room. Dashed awkward. Better to have the guests sit and be served with a regular soup bowl, I think."

Lady Atterley turned a squelching eye on him. "Do be quiet, Peter, and drink your soup."

Desmond lifted his napkin to his lips and whispered to Samantha. "He puts me in mind of your worm."

"What worm?"

"The one on your hook when you're fishing. Yes, poor old Peter got swallowed all right."

Samantha looked at Lord Atterley squirming beside his wife and tried to suppress a giggle, then choked on her soup and indulged in a fit of coughing. Lord Desmond, all grave solicitude, placed her cup on a table and handed her his handkerchief.

"Oh, my dear," said Lady Atterley. "Did you spill something on that lovely dress?"

"Oh, no," breathed Samantha. "I am quite all right."

"You were laughing so. Whatever did Lord Desmond say?"

"Fishing. We were talking about fishing."

"Yes," Desmond added. "I was saying that this was a good season for it."

When Lady Atterley had turned her puzzled gaze away, Samantha returned Desmond's handkerchief and whispered ferociously, "Odious creature! How could you put me into such whoops?"

Amusement lurked in his eyes. "I couldn't have you thinking an evening spent with me could be dull, you know."

Lady Atterley had not been wrong about her lord's generosity and she prided herself on setting a good table. The visitors did full justice to the meal set before them. The second course consisted of buttered crab, kippered herring and perch served in a mushroom sauce. It was followed by a side of beef, yorkshire pudding, chipped mutton fried with parsnips, pheasant pie and several side dishes, including a delicious spinach casserole and a kidney pie. Samantha partook only lightly of each dish, but by the time the sweetmeats were put before her she had to refuse and only tasted a few grapes.

When she could press no more food upon the satiated company, Lady Atterley retired with the ladies to the drawing room, leaving the men to their port and cigars.

Awed by anyone who could fashion such a garment with her own hands, Emily questioned Matilda about details. "That tatted edging is so fine," she declared.

Matilda said she had done it with a special shuttle and offered to show it to Emily. Emily assented and the two took themselves off.

Lady Atterley looked pleased. "I knew they would go on well together. They will soon be the best of friends."

"Yes," Samantha said, not unmindful of Lady Marlowe's warning. "Well, now," said her hostess, "I suppose your banns will be posted soon."

"Banns?"

"Announcing your betrothal." Lady Atterley shook a reproving finger at her. "Now don't be missish! To Lord Desmond, of course."

"Oh, no, Lady Atterley, they will not be posted. That is—you mistake. I am not betrothed to Lord Desmond."

Lady Atterley rolled her eyes in a knowing manner. "Nonsense, my dear! You've put the town on its ears. Everyone is talking about your conquest."

"Conquest? I have made no conquest."

"You are quite right not to boast of such an achievement. It would be most unbecoming. But you can be quite frank with me."

"I assure you, Lady Atterley, I am not betrothed to Lord Desmond."

"Oh, well, now, dear, don't fret so! You will soon have him in your pocket!"

"I will not!" Samantha cried, and almost stamped her foot.

"But of course you will. Just keep going on as you are. I can tell by the way he looks at you that you will soon pull it off!"

"I don't want him in my pocket!"

"Why, of course you do! And you need not be ashamed! Any girl would. Why, I understand he is one of the warmest men in England. At least his father is, and Lord Desmond is so fortunate to be an only son.''

"That does not signify!"

"No, I suppose not. For I understand the marquis was left quite a large independence by his godfather, the earl of Cambridge. Anyway, the duke can't last very long, you know. For he is always ill and staying away from the assemblies. Just think! You will soon be the duchess of Duval!"

Lady Atterley rattled on, and Samantha, overcome with embarrassment, was powerless to stop her.

"Have you seen Somerset? But of course you have. And I shall look forward to an invitation to visit when you are established there. I understand it is absolutely magnificent!"

"My dear Lady Atterley." Samantha spoke as calmly as her turbulent emotions would allow. "How can I impress upon you that I am *not* betrothed—nor do I have any desire to be betrothed to Lord Desmond!"

"Now, child, don't get yourself into a pucker! You don't have to boggle at plain speaking with me! I am well acquainted with the ambitions of a young unattached lady. But you are right not to wear your heart on your sleeve. Just keep denying the thing till you bring it off."

"Lady Atterley—"

"Now, now, take that look off your face! I promise I won't say a word. Not until you've succeeded. And I'll help you."

"Really, you needn't—"

"Nonsense! I'll be glad to. It always helps when an outsider comments to your intended about your beauty and accomplishments. By the by, what are your accomplishments? Do you sing or play the spinet? Shh! I hear the men coming. Well, now, have you gentlemen imbibed sufficiently? Oh, Lord Desmond, Samantha is so charming. I was just complimenting her on that lovely gown she wore to the Ashton's ball.''

Back at Grosvenor Square, Samantha could hardly wait until the door had closed upon them and Emily had gone upstairs. "Please, Lord Desmond, I must speak with you.''

"Of course, Samantha. Let's have a game of chess. Shall I have Brooks bring us something.''

"No. Nothing.''

"Is something wrong, Sam? You've been so strange since dinner.''

"No. Yes. Something is dreadfully wrong.''

"Well, whatever it is, we will soon put it to rights. Come." He took her hand and pulled her into the drawing room, where a small fire still burned. "Now let's talk about it.''

"Lord Desmond, we must put an end to this farce!''

"Farce?''

"This betrothal—this intention—this . . . whatever it is. This tangle we've got into.''

"Tangle? Why, Sam, I thought we were going along famously.''

"Well, we're not. And you must tell your mother immediately that we're not . . . that you're not . . . such a silly expression!—thinking of offering for me. Such a ridiculous idea!''

His look was suspicious. "You did not think it so ridiculous when first we discussed it.''

"Well, I think so now. And it must end. I will not have the whole town thinking I am setting my cap for you!''

"Oh. I begin to see. Did Lady Atterley with some slip of her unguarded tongue make a comment that set your hackles up?''

"A comment! How many did she make! And there was nothing unguarded about her tongue! No veiled innuendoes! No, Lady Atterley does not boggle at plain speaking."

"I see."

"And I could not make her understand that we are not betrothed. That I have no desire to be betrothed. That I would not under any circumstances think of making a conquest of you!"

"Come now! I'm not so bad as all that."

"Oh, no. Not you! You are a nonpareil! The warmest man in England—all set to inherit your father's great wealth and he's got one foot in the grave, you know! To say nothing of the large independence you've already received from some guardian or great-uncle. And you've got a grand estate and your wife will be a duchess and ... oh, this is beyond anything! And what are you laughing at?"

He made an effort to control himself. "Now wait. Let's discuss this calmly."

"Oh, how can I be calm when the whole town is talking about what a cake I'm making of myself over you!"

His lips twitched. "I thought it was a conquest."

"Does it matter? Our relationship."

"But, Samantha, that was just the point."

"It was *not* the point. It was just to make your mother think that we, er, that we were betrothed."

"Exactly."

"Well, just tell her you've changed your mind. This pretence is no longer necessary."

"Aha!"

"What do you mean, 'Aha'?"

"It's no longer necessary now that you've wheedled your way into my parents' good graces."

"*Wheedled* my way!"

"Oh, yes, there's no denying it! My mother dotes on you and my father would be reluctant to lose his chess crony!"

She stared at him. "What do you mean by that?"

"Now that you've accomplished your purpose. Now that you're firmly fixed in London. Your sister is having her come out. And you're not spending your uncle's money."

"Oh, you are abominable!"

"A bargain is a bargain," he insisted stubbornly.

"That's unfair."

"No, indeed, my dear girl. Cast your mind back a few weeks when we were both in such a muddle and we said we would endeavour to serve each other?"

Samantha drew a deep breath and placed both hands to her cheeks. "Oh, I can't stand this!"

"Surely, now that you've served your own purpose, you would not cast me adrift in a sea of tossing caps. You could not be so heartless!"

She chuckled at the smile lurking in his eyes, then frowned.

"Fiddle! You've managed so far to extricate yourself."

"Only by avoiding the sea, my love."

"Don't call me your 'love'!"

"My little reneger then?"

"I am not reneging!"

"Oh, yes you are. Now come, Sam. You know this whole thing happened because I promised my mother I'd stay the season. You can't desert me now."

"Fiddle!" she said again.

"And we were having such fun! Don't let Lady Atterley's wagging tongue get you all upset. *I'm* making the conquest—not you."

"As if anyone would believe that!" She shook her head, but could not help smiling at the implication.

"That's better! You can't hide that dimple. It always gives you away. Now no need for you to worry. I promise I'll make it perfectly clear who's pursuing whom. I'll set it about town that I'm pining with love for that copper-haired Scarborough girl. I'll dog your footsteps. I'll—"

"Oh, be quiet."

But now the storm was over and Samantha's sense of fair play surfaced. She told him that she supposed it wouldn't matter what the people in London thought, since she would soon be returning to Scarborough, anyway.

"That's my girl." He lifted her chin and kissed her lightly on the lips. "There. That's to seal our bargain. Now don't go making a cake of yourself over nothing."

CHAPTER TWELVE

WHEN LADY JULIA MARLOWE gave advice which was ignored and when that advice later proved prophetic, Lady Marlowe was apt to say "I told you so."

Her sister, Sylvia, had not listened when she warned her about becoming intimate with Lenora Atterley. And just last evening when Julia had visited Grosvenor Square, who should she find closeted in the small drawing room with Emily, but Matilda Lindsey, showing her how to do some tatting.

Well, she had warned Sylvia. "Indeed, I told you so. I knew just how it would be." Lady Marlowe turned from her dressing table, where she had been applying a new kind of cream before the duchess joined her. "Sylvia, do stop pacing and sit down."

Her sister paid no heed, so absorbed was she in the perplexities of a son who presented his intended for her approval and then proceeded to dally for weeks without declaring himself. She had told him outright that Samantha had her unqualified approval, and certainly there was no doubt about the duke's approbation. Yet there was no talk of a formal announcement, nor any of posting banns.

"I can't understand it," she said. "They are constantly together."

"Of course they are. I told you how it would be."

"Yes."

"And I know she has her eyes on Mark."

The duchess nodded. "I suppose so. But she's so casual about it. If she goes on this way she'll never bring Mark up to scratch."

"Well, she's nothing like her sister." Lady Marlowe turned to apply more cream to her face.

"But she's quite a taking little thing. So lively. Of course she's not the beauty her sister is."

Lady Marlowe turned, a mound of cream in her hand. "Lenora Atterley! A great beauty?"

"Who said anything about Lenora Atterley?"

"Why, you did so. We were talking about Matilda and I said—"

"Matilda Lindsey? What has she to do with anything? And what is that stuff you're putting on your face?"

"Oh, Sylvia, this new cream is purported to work miracles. Taken from a plant—same plant used by Cleopatra and credited for her great beauty. They say she used the juice on her hair and skin. You apply it like this with upward strokes. Now about Matilda . . ."

"Oh, Julia, will you stop babbling about Matilda Lindsey! I am in such a state about Mark. Samantha has been here for several weeks now and nothing is settled."

"Oh, my dear. I knew from the first that nothing would come of that."

"How can you say such a thing? You know Mark told me he intended to marry her and—"

"He did not. He said that he was thinking of offering for her."

"It amounts to the same thing."

"It does not. And anyway, whatever his plans, he seems to be taking his own good time."

"If that's all you have to say, I'd best be off." The duchess picked up her reticule, adding that she hoped that was a miracle cream, for that's what it would take to make Julia resemble Cleopatra in any way.

Lady Marlowe laughed and begged the duchess not to go off in such a high-handed manner. "After all, I only said just what you've been saying. Besides, I've just thought of something that might help you to bring the whole thing about."

Her sister shrugged and seated herself again.

"I think Mark is about his own distractions," Lady Marlowe continued. "Jasper saw him leaving the theatre the other evening with that Angel D'Angelo hanging on his arm. And it was well after midnight."

"It seems to me that for a married man, Jasper finds himself in strange places at very strange hours," the duchess remarked with a touch of asperity.

"On his way home from White's. Nothing strange about a gentleman leaving his club at that time of night, which is more than I can say for Mark's behaviour. Don't be goosish, Sylvia. I'm only trying to help. The thing is, you need to get them away from London."

"What?"

"Take them where they can't see anybody but each other."

"Where?"

"To Somerset, of course."

"In the middle of the season?"

"And why not?"

"Why, it isn't done. What would people think? What would I say?"

"What you always say. Lord Duval's gout. You know very well, Sylvia, you've been using that excuse for years to get you into or out of whatever you wish."

The duchess was thoughtful. "That might be a very good idea."

"Of course it is. At Somerset, Mark's actress and Samantha's beaux will be quite unavailable."

"Quite." Her sister's eyes sparkled. "Oh, Julia, that is a capital idea. We'll go down on Mark's yacht. It's only a day's sail down the Thames. Let's see. I'll ask young Travis for Emily. Good. Lord Billington will be out of her pocket. And I'll ask Jasper and Melissa."

"Oh, yes." Lady Marlowe smiled. "The children will love it."

"Not the children. We want this to be a quiet romantic holiday to bring Mark to the point, you understand." Jasper's children were such brats, she thought, they might well turn Mark off matrimony altogether.

The duchess said she would cancel all engagements for the following week, as they would leave this Sunday and return on the following one.

Lady Marlowe said that would be a very good thing, as they would then miss Matilda Lindsey's birthday party.

Lady Sylvia was surprised to find her son quite amenable to her plan to remove to Somerset. Had she but known it, Mark was excessively pleased that she had suggested it.

When the proposed visit was broached to Samantha, she was delighted. She was, she admitted to herself, much more a country than a city girl. And as delightful as she had lately found London society, she was glad of a respite. Besides, she felt a keen desire to see Somerset House. She regretted missing Matilda's party, but there was little she could do about it. She did press upon Lord Scarborough the importance of his attendance, just so the poor girl would have one person with whom she felt comfortable.

"And I saw you did make her comfortable at the dinner party. You are so kind, Uncle."

"Dash it, Sam. This is outside of enough. Not only do I have to escort and balance when you're here. Now you want me to go to some other frippery when you ain't here. That don't hardly seem fair."

"But look, Uncle, we'll be away the whole week. You won't have to attend any other affairs."

"Well, that's a jolly good thing. Very good notion of the duchess's—posting down to Somerset. You'll get a good rest. And so will I," he added under his breath.

"Only this one party. Promise?"

"All right, I promise."

"And don't forget some trinket. It's her birthday, you know."

"Now, Sam, you know you've no need to tell me what's proper."

I certainly don't, thought Samantha as she watched him depart. Indeed, it might have been well to warn him against anything expensive. Uncle Stanley was inclined to be extravagant.

Samantha found herself looking forward to the trip. It would be delightful to see Somerset and to sail there on a yacht.

EARLY SUNDAY MORNING the whole party was driven down to the dock to board Mark's yacht, *The Pelican.* There was one big ship, several barges and one other yacht moored at the dock, but *The Pelican*, sleek and shiny, stood out among them. It seemed small when viewed from the dock, but when Samantha boarded it, she found it quite spacious.

Her grace gathered all into the dining quarters for coffee and rolls, promising an early and sumptuous lunch. Samantha heard the crewmen calling one another, felt the ship give a bump and a lurch, and soon they were sailing swiftly down the river.

"Now," said the duchess, "who'd like to join in a game of bridge? Samantha?"

"Oh, no," Samantha cried. "I want to go up on deck. I wouldn't miss this for the world." Then, feeling that she might have been rude, she added, "Well, if you need a fourth...?"

The duchess said she had forgot this was Samantha's first trip, and of course she would want to see all the sights. Melissa and Jasper would play against the duke and the duchess.

Desmond took Samantha's hand and led her on deck, where they were joined by Emily and Arthur. However, in spite of his nautical attire, Arthur proved to be a very poor sailor. He found himself quite unwell before they were an hour downstream, and retired to a bunk in one of the cabins. Uncomfortable over what the wind and spray were doing to her hair, Emily soon sought her own cabin.

After they had passed London, the water became much clearer and was relatively free of debris. Samantha revelled in the fresh clean air and the beauty of the countryside: the wide expanse of land beyond the riverbank, the rolling green hills, the clumps of trees and, here and there, a carefully cultivated field.

She stood holding the rail, loving the roll of the ship beneath her feet, the feel of the wind and spray on her face. "I rather like this mode of travel," she told Desmond. "No rough dusty roads to be traversed. No posting stations to change horses."

"True," he agreed. "But the difficulty is that the Thames does not flow everywhere."

"You're right. You could never get to Scarborough by this route."

"You could get to France, though."

"Oh? I thought you had to travel to Dover?"

"But you can also sail to the mouth of the river, around the cove and across the channel."

"Have you ever done that?"

"Often. You don't think I keep a yacht just to sail up and down the Thames."

"How long does it take? I mean to get to France?"

"Several days. But it's a beautiful trip. I have often thought, should I through some unfortunate circum-

stance find myself with a bride, it would make a very
pleasant honeymoon trip.''

Samantha was thoughtful. ''Several days. Wouldn't you
get bored? You couldn't get out and walk or ride. I should
think you'd get tired just looking at scenery.''

''On a honeymoon?''

She looked up to see a teasing glint in his eyes, his lips
curving in a half smile. She looked quickly downward as
she caught the full import of his question.

''Let me assure you, my little innocent, on a honeymoon there are more interesting things to do than watch
scenery.''

''Oh, you are impertinent!''

He laughed. ''Have I shocked you, Miss Prim and
Proper?''

''No, you have not shocked me. And I am not prim.''
But she felt herself blush to the roots of her hair. There was
nothing prim about the way she felt as she watched his full
mouth curve against his white teeth. She imagined how it
would be to feel those lips against hers, and she was thoroughly ashamed.

He looked down at her. ''I believe I did shock you.''

''No, indeed, you did not. And if you keep dwelling on
honeymoons, one of these days you will find yourself
firmly shackled to some horrible managing female.''

''Ah, but I am not addicted to managing females, only
to copper-haired innocents.''

''And blue-eyed blondes, and redheads, and raven-
haired beauties,'' she cried, and was glad to see him give a
little start. At last she had managed to give him a set-down.
He had no chance to retort, for just then a steward appeared, announcing lunch.

It was quite dark by the time they docked, and she was
able to see very little. They were guided down the ramp by
lamplight and handed into a very unusual vehicle. It was
built like a wagon, but much longer and wider. The front

portion consisted of several rows of comfortable seats and the back was flat, affording ample space for their luggage.

"A contraption Mark dreamt up," the duke explained to Samantha. "It was made by Kelsey, a wheelwright in London, but it was designed by Mark. It was better, he said, than the several carriages needed to convey guests from his yacht. The house is quite a distance from the dock, you know."

"This is a clever and very comfortable conveyance," Samantha said. "Imagine Mark thinking of it."

"Oh, he's always got Kelsey constructing a special curricle or something to his own design. Mark likes anything that has wheels." His grace added that it was good to be home and he thought Samantha would enjoy Somerset.

She agreed and peered into the darkness, trying to see where they were going.

They rode for some time along a winding gravel trail until they reached the house. The doors of the house opened on such a spacious hall that Samantha felt almost as if she were in a cathedral. The floors were of polished stone and the ceiling was high, so high that it afforded an excellent view of the balconies of the two upper stories which curved in an arch around one end of the hall. A wide staircase led to the first landing, then divided into two winding stairs, both leading to the second story. The hall was well lit, with many candles spaced at intervals along the walls. Samantha glimpsed pictures of landscapes and still lifes, mirrors with gilded frames, console tables with bowls of fresh flowers.

The duchess led them into a small salon, where a roaring fire blazed and tea was already laid out. They did not linger long over tea, however, for all were exhausted. The duke said it was the sea air that had them all yawning, and they'd best be off to bed.

Samantha paid little heed to the luxurious bedchamber assigned to her. As soon as she was undressed, she climbed into the four poster, snuggled into its downy softness and fell into an untroubled sleep.

She was awakened early the next morning by the sound of pebbles hitting against her window. She jumped out of bed and opened the shutters to find a grinning Desmond staring up at her. "Are you going to sleep all day, lazybones? I thought you were an early riser."

"And I thought you were a late one," she chided. But she felt her heart give a little thump. He looked so fresh and rested, so handsome in his buff riding breeches and matching coat.

"Well, don't just stand there. Come on down. I want to show you around. Dress for riding, and hurry."

Samantha turned to see Jenny come in with a large pitcher of hot water. In a few moments, she was washed and dressed in a light tan riding habit. She was glad now that Uncle Stanley had made her buy it. She tied her hair back with a matching riband and ran down the stairs to where Desmond was waiting. He took her through a side door to a wide verandah, near which two horses stood saddled and ready.

He handed her the reins of a pretty little chestnut mare and said as if in introduction, "Lady, this is Samantha Scarborough. Miss Scarborough—Pretty Lady."

Samantha bowed in acknowledgement.

"Do you like her?" He said it lightly, but he was like a small boy asking if his present pleased.

"Of course I like her. Hello, Pretty Lady. You are beautiful." She stroked the mare's nose and cried, "Oh, I need some sugar."

Desmond produced a lump from his pocket and Samantha fed it to the horse, talking coaxingly all the time.

"I knew you two would go on well together. And now that you are friends, up you go," he said as he lifted her up into the saddle.

It was a beautiful morning. The dew was still on the grass and the sun barely peeking over the horizon. Samantha felt exhilarated and happy as she turned her mare to follow Desmond.

He did show her everything, as if it were imperative that she know every inch of the place where he had spent his boyhood. They rode past the sweeping cultivated lawns and the carefully planted flower beds and formal gardens of Somerset House to the places he had haunted as a boy. They visited the grove of trees where he had played Robin Hood with the village boys. Then they crossed the moor and went down the hill to a hollowed-out cave where as pirates, he and Peter, the gardener's son, had stashed their treasure. Finally, they made their way down the gravel path to the Thames, where *The Pelican* was docked.

"Did you play on the Thames?" she asked.

"Peter and I built a raft once, but we got caught in an undertow and almost drowned, and Father forbade us the river."

They galloped along the Thames for a while, then rode back on the gravel path. When they'd neared the house, Desmond dismounted and lifted Samantha down. "I want to show you the tree house Peter and I built in that old oak behind the kitchen garden."

It was still there, perched high among the limbs of the spreading oak.

"Do you mean it has borne the ravages of wind and rain for all those years?" Samantha asked as she gazed up at it.

"All those years! I'm not in my dotage yet, girl. And Peter and I were quite capable carpenters." He turned and said, smiling, "I'll walk the horses to the stable. Want to come?"

Samantha declined and sat on the bench that leaned against the oak to wait his return. She looked again at the old tree house! Amazing that it was still there. What fun they must have had, sitting high in the tree, being swayed by the breeze.

Samantha sat up and looked around. It was very secluded; even the kitchen garden was blocked from view by the high trellis of the rose arbour.

She looked up again, studying the branches. Then, without hesitation, she stepped on the bench, grasped a low branch and hoisted herself up into the tree. Bitterly regretting, as she had many times before, the dictates of fashion that put breeches on men and not on women, she gathered up the skirt of her riding habit and began the steady climb upward.

It was not too difficult, for the limbs were like stair steps. But she was impeded by her skirts and was breathing heavily by the time she reached the little structure. She was not surprised to find it remarkably well designed. How like Mark! It was securely fastened in the massive boughs of the old oak tree. It consisted of a small enclosure fashioned of various-sized boards and planks and a balcony just large enough for two small boys. She squeezed herself onto the balcony and looked down and around. Delightful! Though she felt herself hidden by the leaves, she had a good view of the surrounding land. There was the moor they had ridden across to the cave, there were two cows grazing in a meadow and there was Mark, making his way from the stable. He walked with a strong steady gait over ground so familiar to him. Here he had grown up, as had his father and grandfather before him. And—the thought rather startled her—here his child would grow. She pictured a small replica of Mark rambling about, hiding in the cave, sitting here in the tree house his father built. How she could love that grubby little boy with Mark's dark hair and eyes! She stopped—apalled at herself. If she were not careful, she would become one of those silly, manoeuvring, cap-setting females whom she so detested.

She was not aware that Mark had reached the grove until she heard him calling.

"Sam! Samantha! Where are you?"

He looked so frantic stalking about down there that she giggled. He looked up. "Sam! How the devil did you! What are you doing up there?"

"Inspecting your tree house."

"Get down this instant! You'll fall!"

"Oh, no. It's quite sturdy, just as you said."

"Samantha! Please. Somebody might see you."

"You didn't see me. If I hadn't laughed—"

"Samantha!" He glanced toward the house, then back up at her with such perturbation that she burst out laughing.

"It's lovely up here. I just might stay for hours and hours."

"You little..." He gritted his teeth. "Will you come down, or shall I come after you?"

"I don't think there's room for both of us."

"Vixen!" He reached for the limb to swing himself upward, but the small branch which had so easily supported Samantha's weight broke under his and he toppled backward to the ground.

"Oh, Mark! Are you hurt?" Samantha, instantly contrite, scrambled down. Her foot slipped on a lower branch and she fell, rolling awkwardly beside him.

His stillness frightened her. She sat up immediately and touched her hand to his chest to feel his heartbeat.

He clasped her hand and murmured, "Bury me under the old oak tree, where vainly I strove to rescue a maiden in distress."

"Oh, you! I wasn't in distress." She jerked her hand away. "I thought you were hurt!"

She started to rise, but he sat up quickly, seizing her by the shoulders. "And I thought you had more sense than to climb a tree. I ought to shake you until—" He stopped.

Samantha sat transfixed, caught by the intensity of those dark eyes that seemed to search her face. Dimly she was aware of the stillness, a bird singing and an answering one singing in her heart, the throbbing of her pulse as his arms tightened on her shoulders and his lips pressed against hers. She yearned to touch his face, to run her fingers through his hair.

She felt the grip on her shoulders loosen, as his hands became gently caressing and slipped downward to encircle her waist. He pulled her close, and instinctively she nestled against his muscular chest, breathing in the smell of tobacco and shaving soap mingled with green grass and flowers—the sweet fragrance of blooming living things.

"Samantha, my sweet," he murmured.

Her senses reeled as he traced light kisses upon her neck and throat. The song in her heart became a pulsing melody that surged and vibrated in a wild crescendo throughout her whole being. Then his lips claimed hers in a passionate plea so intense that she was powerless to resist. She wound her arms around his neck, clutched at his thick hair and fervently returned his kiss.

She felt him tense, then gently push her away. Coming out of her daze she looked up at him, and was confused, then embarrassed, by the astonishment in his face.

Oh, she was . . . had behaved like a common . . . trollop! Oh, Lord! What must he think of her? Trying to compose herself, she hurriedly got to her feet and started away.

"Samantha! Wait!" Mark rushed after her and caught her hand. His feelings were in turmoil. Samantha! Never had he felt such a hunger for any woman. And he had seen the same hunger mirrored in Samantha's eyes. And never had he felt so much passion, or so much promise, as in the fervour of her responsive kiss. A lady didn't . . . couldn't . . .

But Samantha had responded with passion and longing. So alive. So free.

Samantha's eyes were downcast and she tried to pull away from him. Gently he turned her to face him. He was as confused as she, but he knew he wanted her never to turn away from him, or to be frightened of him, or to be ashamed. He wanted to say something of this to Samantha.

But he couldn't. This emotion was too new to him. He needed time to sort out his feelings, lest he act rashly and lose something that was infinitely precious. He tilted her chin and touched her lips lightly and tenderly with his own, and tried to speak calmly.

"You can't go anywhere looking like that."

Still bewildered, she stared down at herself. "Like what?"

"Looking like—like— Good God, Samantha, nobody'd ever believe you just fell out of a tree!"

She stood motionless while he smoothed her hair and brushed the leaves from her riding habit.

"That's better. Now turn around and let me get the back."

"Ouch!" She turned back to him, eyes flashing. "How dare you! That was no brush! That was a slap on my...on my..."

"That'll teach you not to go climbing trees!" He grinned at her, and some of their easy camaraderie was restored.

When they had walked sedately up to the house, they found the duke on the verandah with his pipe and book. He remarked upon Desmond's early rising, and when Mark explained that he had just been showing Samantha around, his grace muttered a noncommittal "I see."

The duchess also was surprised to see Mark up so early, but said he did exactly right, showing Samantha about the grounds, and soon she must show Samantha the house.

"No, I'd better let Swanson do it. She knows the work-ings of the place better than I."

So, promptly after breakfast, Mrs. Swanson, the plump and agreeable housekeeper, gave Samantha a tour, point-ing out such minute details as the store of the linens and china, the particular polish for the silver. The underser-vants bowed to Samantha as if welcoming a new mistress, and she began to feel very uncomfortable, especially when Mrs. Swanson showed her "the young master's wing."

"It's complete to the touch, as you can see. It's the young master's now. But, of course, if the duke should, if he, that is, if the duchess should ever find herself alone, then this would be the dowager's quarters and the young master would take the duke's place. Maybe it's too mas-culine for your taste, but you... Well, that is, if the young master should take a bride she could furnish it to her taste."

These not-so-subtle references, which she didn't know how to counteract, troubled Samantha, and she was glad when the tour was over.

The week was an enjoyable holiday for all of them. Carefully attended by Jasper, Melissa sat for long hours on the terrace, complacently knitting tiny pink and blue gar-ments. Even Emily seemed not to miss London, but went contentedly about with Arthur in their old companion-able way. There was croquet on the lawn in the afternoon, and in the evenings there was bridge and chess and com-fortable talk in the drawing room.

One morning Mark told Samantha to wear something cool. They would not take the horses out—he had a sur-prise for her. She appeared in a yellow dimity morning dress, rather fetching with its ruffled border, and Des-mond gazed at her approvingly.

She was surprised to see another strange vehicle, with one high seat in front and several small cases in back.

"Kelsey made it. For my fishing expeditions."

"Oh, Mark! Are we going fishing? How delightful! I haven't fished since Papa..."

"I know. Climb in."

"The Thames?" she inquired.

"No, indeed. The Singing Brook—where the water is fresh and sparkling."

When he lifted her down from the cart, Samantha caught her breath. "Oh, it is lovely! The Singing Brook really sings. You know, that gurgling sound that comes from the spring. Why didn't we ever name our stream at Scarborough? We just call it the stream!"

"Very unromantic of you."

"Yes. I'll name it as soon as I get back."

The cases contained worms and fishing tackle. One was packed with straw and great hunks of ice from the ice house.

"You're very clever to design such a cart."

"Yes, I know. Here's your tackle and rod."

When she cast her line into the stream, Desmond looked at her admiringly. "You are a strange lady, Sam. So businesslike about your fishing. You just grabbed that worm, stuck it on the hook and cast it in, waiting for some poor unsuspecting fish."

"You're teasing me."

"Indeed I'm not. Do you know how many ladies squeal at the sight of a worm?"

"I told you. Papa often took me fishing. I love it."

"I see."

Desmond caught two fish, Samantha one.

"This is so peaceful," she breathed. "I could stay here forever."

"Could you now?" He said it softly, and there was a strange look in those dark eyes.

She bit her lip. "I mean, it's such a lovely lazy day. You don't want to move."

"I see."

Now what kind of look was that? Teasing or mocking or . . . She felt a sharp pull on her line.

"Oh, Mark. I've got a big one. Help me. Don't let him get away." She felt the rod almost snatched from her and grasped it tighter, unconsciously stepping knee-deep into the water. She would have fallen had not Mark put his arms around her and pulled her back onto dry land. The rod slipped from her fingers and she gasped. "He got away! He got away!"

Mark's arms were still around her, and she looked up to see him laughing.

"You silly gudgeon! You almost fell headlong into the water and all you can say is 'He got away.' "

Suddenly she was conscious of his nearness, his hard body pressing against her own, making her feel weak and alive and curiously yielding. She looked at his lips, so tantalizingly close to hers.

"Oh, please," she whispered, wanting him to kiss her again.

He drew a deep breath and abruptly released her. Struggling to regain his composure, Desmond spoke more harshly to hide his confusion. "Look at you. And now you're getting me all wet. Sit down and let me take off those shoes. Damme, if you're not falling out of trees, you're falling into creeks."

Numbly she watched him remove her shoes, pour the water out and set them aside to dry. *Samantha Scarborough, you wanton! Pull yourself together.*

"Don't look so woebegone. No harm done," said Desmond. "Just take off your stockings and let them dry, and spread your dress out a bit."

She forced herself to smile. "I'm not woebegone. I'm not such a goose! And I'll pull off my stockings when your back is turned.

He obediently turned his back, and by the time she had wrung out her stockings and hung them to dry, she was quite herself again.

"Well," she announced, "since I'm already in disgrace I might as well enjoy myself." She spread her skirts about her, but deliberately stuck her bare feet into the cool water.

"Samantha, you are quite incorrigible."

"Well, when I went fishing with Papa I often used to wade in the stream."

He shook his head, staring at her wriggling toes. "Can't say I don't envy you—here I am in these hot boots. Sure you didn't fall in the water deliberately? You're being very unladylike, you know."

She chuckled. "I know. Please don't tell. I should be in such disgrace."

"Oh, I won't tell. For I should be in disgrace myself."

"I do hope I have not ruined this dress. Do you think it will be quite all right?"

"I think so."

"The thing is, at Scarborough I would have worn some old clothes and it wouldn't have mattered in the least."

"You stop running around in old clothes!"

"What?" She was startled by his tone.

"Do you know I thought you were a servant wench when I met you at Scarborough? You could get into some dangerous situations looking like that. A man would think..."

"And who would see me in Scarborough?"

"I saw you!"

"Oh, pooh, that was most unusual. Nobody comes—"

"Samantha, I forbid it!"

She looked up, shocked at his tone.

"With your carefree ways, you'd better take pains to look like a lady. It makes a difference," he muttered.

"Well, while you're drying I might as well get out the lunch."

A little puzzled at his gruff manner, Samantha said nothing.

The cook had prepared an excellent lunch, and by the time they had consumed it, they had regained their old easy companionship. And by the time they tired of fishing, Samantha's clothes were dry and she could return to the house without fearing censure.

CHAPTER THIRTEEN

THEY FOUND LONDON hot and dusty after the fresh green fields of Somerset. But they also found many waiting cards, and the duchess said they would soon be in the swirl again.

Lady Marlowe visited on the following afternoon and no sooner was she ushered into the drawing room than Brooks appeared, saying that Lord Scarborough was in the small salon and wished a private word with his elder niece. After a word of greeting to Lady Marlowe, Samantha excused herself.

Before she was out of hearing, however, she caught Lady Marlowe's query, "How did it go?" And the duchess's disgruntled reply that for all that was accomplished, they might as well have stayed at home. This surprised Samantha, for the duke appeared to be in excellent spirits. Indeed, he had not uttered one word of complaint. Perhaps he was one of those brave people who kept his miseries to himself.

As she entered the salon, all thoughts of the duke were banished from her mind. For, as Lord Scarborough turned toward her, she could see he was in very poor spirits, indeed.

"Sam, I don't know what to do. I've got myself in a bit of—a kind of—well, plague take it, a blasted tangle!"

"Is it money, Uncle?" For his harassed expression reminded her of Mr. Simmons that day he had complained about Lord Stanley's expenditures.

"Money?" He looked at her in a blank sort of way.

"Yes. Your debts."

"Oh, good God, no. This ain't the usual. This is the devil of a coil."

"Now, Uncle, just be calm and tell me."

"It ain't that I—well, I know she's a poor little put-upon thing . . . but . . . Dash it—I don't want to marry!"

"Marry?"

"Sam, I'm betrothed."

"Betrothed!" Samantha gasped. "But who—that is, when— How did it happen?"

"Damme, that's just what I'd like to know." He took a handkerchief from his pocket and mopped his brow.

"To whom are you betrothed, Uncle Stanley?"

"Matilda Lindsey."

Samantha sat down and stared up at him. "You offered for Matilda Lindsey?"

"Oh, no, I didn't offer."

"Then you can't possibly be engaged. First you must offer, and she must accept."

"Well, I didn't and she didn't and I am. That's all I know. I tell you, Samantha, it's the devil of a coil."

She took his hand and drew him down beside her. "There's just some kind of mistake. Now just tell me from the beginning exactly what happened."

"It was a mistake all right. That damned trinket!"

"What trinket?"

"The one you told me to get for Matilda's birthday. Remember?"

"But what—"

"Well, I saw a little ring . . ."

"Oh, Uncle Stanley, no. Surely not a ring!"

"Yes. Just the thing. Turquoise, you know. Like her eyes."

"Uncle Stanley, you know it's not proper to give jewelry to a lady."

"The devil it ain't! I do it all the time. Had a little opera dancer once who said—"

"Opera dancers! That's different."

"Damme, Sam, don't keep getting off the subject. Thing was, I bought this little ring, see? And I gave it to Tilly."

"Tilly?"

"Matilda. And she was gasping over it and I could tell she was pleased, and then that rattle of a sister pounced on us. You know, Sam, she's a deuced pouncing woman and first thing I know—we're betrothed."

"Lady Atterley said you were betrothed?"

"Well, not exactly. What she said was 'Oh, Matilda, you sly young thing, you never said a word,' and then she said what a dashing devil I was, shouting all the time, you know, in that way she has. And then she tells the whole damme room—must have been half of London there—that she knew she could rely upon their discretion because this was not a formal announcement and no banns had been posted yet and—well, there it was. Devil of a coil, I tell you!" He got up, still mopping his brow, and paced around the room.

"Oh, Uncle Stanley." It was all her fault; Mark had warned her. And she had said so smugly that Uncle Stanley would know how to go on. But not with a trickster like Lady Atterley! It was a shame!

"But, Uncle Stanley, couldn't you explain? What did you say?"

"What could I say? With everybody standing there gaping at us! And Tilly, as surprised as me, standing there with her head down. Couldn't embarrass her even more, you know."

"I suppose not."

"Not that I had the chance. What with Lady Atterley pulling me aside and Peter just standing there. That man's a jellyfish, Sam. Never said a word while that wife of his prattled on about posting banns."

"Posting banns! Uncle, you didn't!"

"No, got out of that one. At least for the time being. Told her I couldn't think of such a thing till you and Emily— My wards, you know—had to get you off first. Devilish good thing you ain't connected yet. Now what? It ain't funny, Sam, you know, indeed, it isn't."

Samantha stifled a laugh and threw her arms around him. "Never mind. We'll get you out of this muddle somehow."

"You think we can, Sam?"

"I'll talk to Matilda."

"Matilda! She ain't the one. It's that rattlepate sister."

"You're right," she agreed. "I'll talk to Lady Atterley."

He looked sceptical. "She ain't an easy one, you know. Talks around things."

Samantha nodded, remembering her last conversation with Lady Atterley. Lord Scarborough suggested he accompany her. It would take both of them to pull the thing off.

Samantha shook her head. "No, I think you've pulled off quite enough. Why don't you, er, aren't they racing somewhere?"

"Doncaster."

She suggested that he go to the races. She could manage it better if he was out of town.

He looked at her imploringly. "Sam, I'll be eternally grateful if you can get me out of this, and not embarrass Matilda, you understand. Hate to have it all over town that she was jilted or something."

Samantha promised that she would find some graceful way of releasing them both. She and Lady Atterley.

"If you do that, Sam, I'll give you most anything."

"Ha! That's no kind of promise."

"Eh?"

"You do that anyway." She held his hand against her cheek. "It's time we did something for you."

"Well, I'd be obliged if you just didn't get yourselves engaged until we get out of this tangle."

She promised and he took himself off, saying he would post down to Doncaster that very afternoon.

Samantha set off for Atterley House in Berkeley Square, determined to have no roundaboutation from Lady Atterley. That woman had seized upon Uncle Stanley's generosity to trick him into a betrothal. Well, Lady Atterley was not the only one who did not boggle at plain speaking. Anticipating the interview, Samantha planned to do some plain speaking of her own.

She did not have that chance. She was informed by the butler that the family had departed for a fortnight's visit to the Atterley estate. Miss Lindsey, it seemed, was unwell, and Lady Atterley thought the country air might revive her.

Samantha felt strongly that it was Lady Atterley's purpose to circumvent any interviews, thus giving her party guests ample time to spread the rumour of the engagement. Well, Sam vowed, that would not signify. Still, there was nothing she could do until they returned.

When she reached Duval House, she was handed a note from Lord Rutherford. He was glad she had returned to town and they could resume their morning rides.

Samantha smiled. It was good of Lord Rutherford to mount her on his Miss Silver. She liked the little mare and she did enjoy the rides in the park, though of course they could not compare with her rides at Scarborough or Somerset.

Somerset. Samantha thought of the morning rides through the beautiful grounds with Desmond, exploring his childhood home, talking, laughing together, and... Samantha felt herself blush as she remembered the touch of Mark's hand, his kiss. Oh, she was behaving like a lovesick schoolgirl! She must not presume too much. Didn't she know of Lord Desmond's scandalous reputation with women? She had heard of that long before she had met him. *You'd best guard your emotions,* she warned herself, *and learn to enjoy the company of other men.*

And, in truth, Lord Rutherford was a most pleasant companion. She frowned. Desmond had seemed quite vexed that she might be becoming too intimate with Rutherford. But . . . oh, fiddle! What did a ride in the park signify?

Next morning, just before Rutherford arrived, she slipped on the green riding habit and tied her hair back with a wide green ribbon. She would not wear the hat and veil even if she was in London. She might not have a wild gallop, but at least she would feel the breeze through her hair.

Lord Rutherford's eyes lit with appreciation as he helped her into the saddle. "Miss Scarborough, I find you magnificent. And courageous."

"Courageous?"

"To ride bareheaded in Hyde Park."

"Oh. I am sorry. I hadn't thought. That is, do you mind?"

"Mind?" He mounted his horse and smiled down at her. "I think it enchanting—that green riband through those copper curls. I think perhaps you will start a new fashion."

She laughed. "I must confess I had thought not of fashion, but of freedom."

"Ah! That is what I like. A free-spirited woman. Come, we will have a fine gallop."

They did have rather a good gallop, for it was early and the park was almost deserted. However, after about an hour, it was filled with the usual stylish vehicles as members of the ton began their inevitable parade. Lord Rutherford was acquainted with many people and often they stopped by a carriage to exchange greetings or chat with some friend.

They had paused by a barouche, and Lord Rutherford was engaged in a political discussion with the rather elderly gentleman occupant, when Samantha's attention was attracted to an approaching vehicle. In fact, many eyes were focused upon it, for it made a very striking picture. A high-perched phaeton with a pair of matched bays, it was of the same bay colour as the mares, and its wheels and trim were as black as their manes and tails. The matching colours were also carried out in the attire of the lady driver. She wore a bay-hued dress braided with black, and a soft veil of the same bay shrouded the high crown of her black hat. The face and figure were those of the same dark beauty who had occupied the adjoining box at Ascot.

Samantha stared at one of the mares. It looked like... But, no, it couldn't be. But it certainly looked like her own dear Bonnie. As they drew nearer to her, the horse whinnied as if in greeting, and Samantha recognized the tiny jagged scar between the eyes—a scar caused by a broken fence when Bonnie was just a filly. It was all Samantha could do not to reach out and touch her.

The phaeton moved slowly past, as if the lady wished to afford everyone a good look. Lord Rutherford, who had bid goodbye to his friend, looked after it.

"Angel D'Angelo. An actress."

"Yes. I know." *Bonnie. That was Bonnie!*

"Cuts quite a dash in her new phaeton with the matched bays."

"Yes."

"A gift, I understand, from her lover." The grey eyes slanted toward Samantha.

"Oh?" Her voice was barely audible.

The grey eyes looked again toward her, then quickly away. "Quite an expensive toy. He must think a good deal of her."

"Yes." *Desmond*. How clearly she remembered Clinton's whispered words: "A good match, my lord."

So that was why he had chosen Bonnie! To secure a matched pair of bays for his lady love.

"You look a little flushed. Are you ill?" Lord Rutherford's voice was all concern.

Did he know? There had been something in his tone when he said "her lover." She gave him what she hoped was a bright smile. "Oh, no, I'm quite fine. It's just that, well, the park is so crowded now and..."

"Quite so. Shall we leave the horses at the stable? My carriage is there."

"No. Oh, yes. That will be fine." Anything. She had to think, must pull herself together. She remembered the look of intimacy that had passed between Desmond and that woman at the races. In her heart she had known then what was so clear now. They were lovers! Lady Atterley had said she was a nobody—born in a workhouse. What did that signify? Even a wilderness produced beautiful flowers, and this woman was a flower of exquisite beauty. How could he not love her? He must, for when he could have chosen Black Knight, he was thinking only of a gift for her.

She realized that they had already reached the stable, and Rutherford was saying something to her. With great effort she willed herself to concentrate.

Yes, it had been a beautiful ride. Such a beautiful horse, Miss Silver. Perhaps soon they could again ride.

All the way home she laughed a good deal, hardly knowing what was said. She felt weighed down. Angry! Betrayed! Yet she knew she had no right to feel so. Somerset. She would not think of Somerset, where they had been so close. They had made a bargain. She was only a screen to protect him while he...oh, how had she let her feelings get out of control? How could she have responded to that meaningless kiss? How could she have imagined that his eyes were caressing her? Not after they had feasted on such beauty!

Yes, she told Lord Rutherford, she would love to see the museum. "Are the marbles from Greece really very damaged?" She must get hold of herself. No one, certainly not Desmond, must ever suspect.

LORD DESMOND STOOD on the steps outside the Duval home in Grosvenor Square and frowned. Samantha was again out.

His mother, a worried look on her face, had questioned him. "Mark, darling, have you quarrelled?"

No, he assured her, they had not quarrelled.

"Then what is amiss?"

"Nothing," he insisted. "Nothing is amiss." But her worried look persisted. She knew as well as he that he was lying.

What the devil was it? They had been going on so well. Now, two times out of three, when he called she was not at home. And when they were together she was different somehow. Detached. Not that she had ever been a clinging vine. But the old camaraderie, the effortless good times when they were together, seemed to have vanished. What had got into the girl? Damme, they had made a bargain! She should be available more often. There she was, careering off with . . . Why, who the devil was she off with? His mother had not volunteered and he did not like to ask. Not good to appear too anxious.

But what the blazes had got into Samantha? Had she found somebody she particularly liked? He clenched his fist, sickened. No, irritated! They had made a bargain, and by God, she should stick to it.

A carriage drew up behind Desmond's tilbury, and Arthur Travis got out. Damned macaroni. Didn't he know frog buttons were passé? Somebody should give him a hint to try Weston's for his coats.

"Emily's not here," he informed the young man.

Arthur's face fell. "I have tickets for a jolly good play tonight. Let's see, it's called . . ." He pulled the tickets out of his pocket.

"Don't matter. You're out of luck. She ain't home. Matter of fact, nobody is." Desmond strode to his tilbury and set his horses off at a fast gallop.

Still holding the tickets in his hand, Arthur looked after him. Now what was wrong with Desmond? He seemed quite out of sorts!

Arthur looked down at the tickets, tore them into tiny bits and started to drop them into the gutter. But, noting how spotless were the streets of Grosvenor Square, he hesitated, then stuffed the torn pieces into his pocket. He would throw them disdainfully onto a table in front of a repentant Emily. That is, when he could catch her at home.

Meanwhile, what? Having dismissed his hack, Arthur walked disconsolately toward Piccadilly, trying to decide how best to fill his time. His host and London sponsor was Sir Arthur Harding, his godfather. This elderly gentleman seldom stirred from his house, but had thoughtfully presented his godson with cards of admittance to the various establishments catering to gentlemen of quality. Arthur had once or twice visited Jackson's Pugilistic Parlour, where one could exercise, or if one chose, could go a round or two with a friend. It was to this establishment that Arthur was headed when a luxurious coach rumbled past him.

It passed quite near him, and in the glow of a street lamp, he caught an excellent view of the laughing lady passenger. The laugh and the hair were well-known to Arthur. There was no mistaking Emily Scarborough! The arms on the carriage were those of Lord Billington.

Luckily Jackson's was not far away and Arthur could vent his rage upon a punching bag. He was thus engaged when accosted by an old friend and Eton classmate, Mr. Tom Carpenter.

"Arthur, old fellow! I had no idea you were in town! Why didn't you let me know?"

Rather glad of an excuse to catch his breath, Arthur paused. "Haven't had time. I've been rather busy." No need to explain what he'd been busy doing.

"Pity. We could have gone about together. What are your plans for this evening?"

Learning that Arthur just happened to be free this particular evening, his London friend, who professed to know all the ins and outs, offered to take him about.

They lingered at Jackson's to watch a match between two gentlemen, then attended a cock fight. But the bulk of the evening was spent visiting several taverns for which no card of admittance was needed. The taverns rang with noise and laughter and were packed with persons unknown to them. But they never lacked for company. A familiar-mannered man, or more often a heavily roughed woman smelling of gin and cheap perfume, would greet them heartily. "Good evening, laddies, would you like some company?"

The two gentlemen, anxious to prove they were men, not laddies, and both flush with pocket money, welcomed the newcomers and bought drinks all around. Arthur was more than a little foxed by the time the two friends presented themselves at White's for a little gaming.

Mr. Carpenter had assured his friend that they could play at faro or piquet, games familiar to him, and need not take a turn at the unfamiliar ivories. However, swaying a bit and blinking at the blaze of lights within the house, Arthur was attracted by the rattle of dice at a centre table. He was astounded by the large piles of paper and gold in front of the players. In his befuddled state, it was some time before he recognized that one of the players was the bejeweled Lord Billington. He fastened his gaze upon that figure, and the rage, not quite vented upon the punching bag, began to rise again. He paid little heed to the buzz of conversation around the table, but he came to attention when one of the players addressed Lord Billington.

"Thought you wouldn't make it tonight, Billington. You were rather late."

Billington's mouth stretched into a grin.

"I had an engagement. I had promised a lady I'd take her to see Lady Peyton's Gaming House."

"No lady goes there!" One of the men laughed.

"Not unless she's a daring little minx, as this one certainly is," Lord Billington replied. "And in the right place—or perhaps I should say the wrong place—a lady may behave like a trollop!"

Arthur's fist clenched as the other men roared with laughter.

"And your lady," one asked. "How did she behave?"

"Like a milkmaid behind the barn." Billington went on to explain that once a lady was out of her natural environment, one might be greatly surprised and sometimes greatly rewarded.

Arthur's head pounded and his face felt hot. His fingers itched to grab Billington and thoroughly thrash him. But one did not brawl in a gaming house.

A duel! One could challenge a person to a duel. Fuzzily Arthur searched for the proper way to do this. A glass of wine in the face. But Arthur, at the moment had no wine.

Still the man's insulting, drawling voice went on, and the laughing faces of his listeners swung dizzily before Arthur's eyes. In one blinding flash of fury, Arthur picked up Billington's glass of wine and dashed it into the surprised man's face.

"What the devil!" Lord Billington, choking and wheezing, wine dripping from his elegant evening coat, stood and faced Arthur in as much confusion as anger.

"Name your weapon, sir." Arthur reeled a bit and shook off the hand of his friend Tom, who sought to restrain him.

"Arthur, don't be a fool. What are you about?"

"He has sullied the name of a decent and fair young lady, and he shall answer to me!"

"I named no name," the earl quite honestly pointed out.

"And only you and I shall ever know the name of the lady you have so grossly insulted." Arthur gave Tom such a push that the young man would have fallen had he not been caught by one of the interested spectators. "Your lips shall remain sealed. Name your weapons."

"Yours shall certainly be sealed," gasped Lord Billington, who had noted that his flowered weskit had also been stained by the wine. "I shall seal them with my sword."

Arthur, who did not own a sword, was taken aback but managed to recover. "Swords it shall be!" Tom could certainly procure one somewhere. "And at the time and place of your choosing."

Seeing he could not move Arthur, Tom solicited the help of some of the other gentlemen who appealed to the earl.

"Be reasonable, Billington! Can't you see the boy is drunk? Let him go. Apologize for whatever it was you said."

Tom continued to appeal to Arthur. "Back down, man. Don't be a fool. Tell him you made a mistake or something."

All was to no avail. Lord Billington, who feared the wine stains could not be removed from his clothes, would not give way. And Arthur, who was now enjoying his role of swashbuckling hero, had no intention of spoiling the drama. The duel was set for dawn at Paxton Heath, and the two young gentlemen departed in search of swords.

But first Arthur directed the driver of the hack they would head for Grosvenor Square. The honour of dying for a lady was quite lost if the lady did not know it.

First, just in case, a tearful farewell to Emily.

CHAPTER FOURTEEN

"SAMANTHA! OH, SAMANTHA, do wake up!"

"For goodness sake, Emily!" Samantha tried to pull herself out of a deep sleep. "It's the middle of the night. Whatever is the matter?" Then, seeing that Emily was fully dressed, she cried, "Where are you going?"

"Nowhere. That is, I've been."

"Where?"

"Downstairs with Arthur. He had Brooks bring me a note. He said it was a matter of life and death. And, oh, Samantha, it is! It is! Oh, I'm so frightened. You can't imagine what has happened."

"No, I can't." Samantha yawned. "But if you would be so good as to inform me..."

"Arthur has challenged Lord Billington to a duel."

"What!" Fully awake, Samantha sat up now.

"They are going to fight with swords! Over *me*! Isn't that romantic? Just wait till I tell Elsie Macon!"

Samantha looked suspiciously at her sister. "And just what has provoked this life or death contest?"

"Oh, Lord Billington said some absolutely horrid things about me! Just because I went with him to that gaming house. And that was so mean, for he told me himself that that was what all the more daring ladies did. And Arthur was right there and told him, 'You shall not sully the fair name of the lady I love!' And he threw a glass of wine in his face and—"

"You mean Arthur is going to get himself killed for *that*?"

"Oh, Samantha, don't say that! I shall just die if Arthur is killed. For I do believe I love him. He is so brave. And so chivalrous. 'You shall not sully...'"

"When and where is this duel to be?"

"At the heath at dawn."

"*This* dawn?"

Emily nodded. "Suppose Arthur kills Lord Billington! He would have to flee the country! Samantha, do you think Uncle Stanley would let me flee with him?"

"I assure you I will persuade him to allow you to flee to Australia if you so desire!" Samantha was up now, and reaching for her clothes.

Emily went on, vacillating between horror at the forthcoming duel and joy at being the object of it.

Fully dressed, Samantha paused. She had dressed not knowing what she was going to do, only that she must do something. Uncle Stanley? Never any good in a crisis! Arthur? She did not even know where he lived. To appeal to her hosts would only mean disgrace for Emily.

Desmond! He would know what to do.

She dispatched a sleepy Jenny to obtain Desmond's direction from the Duval butler, and soon, in a hired hack, was on her way there.

Desmond's door was opened by a very surprised Clinton, who seemed reluctant to admit her. She held her head high and spoke in her most authoritative voice. "I must see his lordship immediately, Clinton."

Clinton peered outside at the waiting hack, then stepped aside. "Come in, Miss Scarborough. I will speak to his lordship." He led her to a small library and bid her wait.

Hardly noticing her surroundings, Samantha paced the floor, her mind in a turmoil. Arthur and his playacting! Now see where his theatrics had got him! He would find that one did not play at duelling and with swords! Oh, dear heaven! How could she face Lady Travis if something happened to her only son? And all on account of Emily. What was keeping Desmond?

She heard a door open and a clear feminine voice call out, "Now who could be visiting you at his hour, my love? Clinton, send them away."

Samantha stiffened. There was a muffled exclamation, a door slamming and quick footsteps down the hall.

Desmond came in, hair tousled, shirt half-buttoned, as if he had started to dress and had not yet finished.

"Samantha, what are you doing here?"

Surprised at his obvious anger, she could only stammer, "I—I had to see you."

"At this hour!"

Of course. He resented the intrusion. Frightened at the look in his eyes, she could only repeat herself. "I had to see you."

"You couldn't send for me? You had to come out on the streets of London, alone, at this hour?"

"Oh, that. It's all right. I hired a hack. He's waiting for me."

Desmond turned to a waiting Clinton. "Pay the man off and dismiss him. I'll see Miss Scarborough home."

Clinton went out and Desmond gripped Samantha by her arms, almost shaking her. "Listen to me. Don't you ever, *ever* come out alone at this hour! Do you understand?" His eyes were hard and furious and his fingers dug into her arm. She winced, and he released her and brushed a hand through his hair. "I'm sorry. I . . . it's just that you don't realize the danger. . . ."

Exasperated, she shook back the hood of her coat and stamped her foot. "Danger! You don't know the danger! Will you stop your raving and listen to me!"

He stepped back then and regarded her warily, but with something of amusement in his face. "I see. Who am I to rescue now?"

"What?" Did he know about Arthur?

"The last time I saw you look like that your dog was caught in a trap. Who or what is in distress now?"

"Emily. No, Arthur."

"Both of them?"

"No. Just Arthur. But Emily provoked it. Arthur has challenged Lord Billington to a duel over some silly thing he said about Emily, which I am sure she deserved. And— oh, Mark, they are going to fight with swords and—"

"Swords!"

"Yes, and I know that Arthur has playacted at almost everything, but I don't believe he ever went in for fencing. And it would be the stupidest thing to get himself killed. Oh, Mark. How can I face Lady Travis. Oh, stop them, please. Please, Mark."

"Now, Samantha, pull yourself together. Of course I'll stop them. I'll see Billington right now. Where is Travis?"

She looked at him blankly. "I—I don't know."

"All right. Never mind. I'll find him. Wait. Let me get my coat."

Already Samantha felt relieved. A moment later she was alarmed by the sound of breaking glass—as if a vase had been hurled against a wall. Then another crash, and angry shouts in the same feminine voice she had heard before. The voice was muffled, so that she could not understand the words, but it was certainly clear that someone—some woman—was angry and sought to detain Desmond. His love? Of course—the beautiful woman in white. She was here in his house—in his bedroom.

Samantha felt sick. When she had seen the dark beauty proudly driving Bonnie, a gift from her lover, she had felt hurt and angry. But it was nothing compared to this. To suspect that they were intimate was one thing. To know it was unbearable.

Desmond reappeared, fully dressed, calm and unruffled, as if there had been no angry shouts—as if Samantha's heart had not just broken into a million pieces.

"All set. Let's go." His voice called her back to the immediate problem. "There now, don't look so distressed."

She felt herself tremble as he lifted her hood and tied it under her chin. His expression caught and held her. For even now his eyes seemed to caress her. In spite of her confusion, she felt reassured by his words.

"No need for you to worry. I promise you there will be no duel."

With his own key, Desmond opened the Duval door and slipped Samantha quietly in. Then he went immediately to Lord Billington's, and, ignoring the attempts of that gentleman's valet to detain him, bounded up the stairs to his bedroom.

"Gads, Mark! What the devil do you want?" the irate earl protested. "Do you know the time! And I've got an early appointment."

"Yes, I know. It is that which I have come about."

"Is the tale abroad already?" Lord Billington swung his legs out of bed and sat up. "Oblige me, Mark, that brandy over there on that table."

Mark poured two glasses of brandy and handed one to the earl, who sipped it eagerly. "Damme good stuff, if I do say so myself. So you've already heard about the duel?"

"News travels fast." The marquis, who had seated himself in a chair, stretched his long legs and studied the amber liquid in his glass. "Nasty business. He's rather young, I understand. And you know how people talk."

"Damnation! He challenged me! Damned nigh ruined my coat when he did it! Let 'em talk."

"Well—" Desmond yawned "—you are a good swordsman."

"Damned good! 'Name your weapon,' the young sap-skull yelled. You should have seen his eyes bulge when I said swords!"

"Oh?" Desmond's eyebrows went up. "That surprises me, for I understand he's quite a performer himself."

In the act of refilling his glass, Lord Billington paused. "Fencer?"

Mark shrugged. "I thought you knew."

"How should I know? I don't even know the young fool's name." His hand shook and he spilled a little of the brandy. "Fencer, is he?"

"Quite an actor, and quite skilled, I understand."

"Skilled, eh?"

"Perfectionist. Well-known in university circles."

"Oh." The earl put his glass down and turned nervous eyes toward Desmond.

Desmond yawned, then got up as if to depart. "Oh, well, as long as you know what you're getting into..."

"Oh, hold on there, Mark. I've been thinking. The young lad was pretty well foxed."

"Oh?"

"Yes. I'm sure his head has cleared a bit and he'd probably like to get out of it."

"Think so?"

"Nasty thing, too. You know how people talk."

"True."

"I hate to take advantage of him when he was in his cups. Don't look right. Maybe I ought to just write a note of apology. Reckon that'd do it?"

"It might."

The earl reached for pen and paper, then paused. "Don't even know the young fool's name. He was with Carpenter's boy. Can't say 'Dear Friend of Mr. Carpenter...'"

"Try 'Dear Sir,'" Desmond suggested.

On the street, note in pocket, Desmond hesitated. The apology was no good unless it was accepted. Carpenter. That was the only clue he had to Arthur's whereabouts.

The Carpenter butler, in nightshirt, said no, sir, Mr. Tom was not at home and no, he did not know where he was—he had left early in the evening for Mr. Jackson's Pugilistic Parlour.

Though the hour was late, Jackson's Parlour was well lit. Desmond opened the unlocked door and went in.

Young Tom Carpenter, chin in hand, was seated disconsolately on a bench, watching two figures in the ring. Stripped to the waist and in his stocking feet, Arthur was awkwardly brandishing a sword at a despairing Jackson, who gave him panting instructions.

"No, no, not that way. Watch me. Thrust... parry... thrust."

Watching the contest, Desmond was infinitely glad he had a note of apology in hand.

"I beg your pardon," he said. "But may I interrupt you gentlemen?"

"Gladly," said Jackson, hastily jumping down from the ring.

Arthur, though his instructor was gone, continued the contest, poking at the air and muttering, "Thrust... parry... thrust."

Jackson shook his head. "He ain't ready." Then he turned to Desmond. "What can I do for you, my lord?"

Desmond indicated that it was with Arthur he wished to speak, and, with some difficulty, gained that young man's ear.

"Make it quick," Arthur panted. "I'm readying myself for a duel."

"That is why I have come." Desmond handed Arthur Billington's note. "Lord Billington very much regrets his rash words and extends an apology."

Arthur read the note and thrust it aside. "No," he said, "that will not do."

Tom picked the note up. "Yes, it will. It will do, Arthur. He has apologized. See. All you have to do is write a note saying you accept his apology."

"No," Arthur repeated.

Jackson mopped his brow. "Sir, with all due respect to your fencing ability, I strongly advise you to accept this apology."

"No," Arthur said again. "He has stained the name of my fair lady and—"

"If you persist in this duel," Desmond said sharply, "I fear there will be more stains than that."

Arthur lifted his head defiantly. "Bloodstains, you mean. And be they his or mine, they shall flow to atone for the insults heaped upon—"

"Oh, that was not what I meant," Desmond said quickly. Arthur had been quite correct in his assumption, but now Desmond sought to change the direction of his thinking. "I meant more stains upon the name of the fair lady. After all, a duel will create more scandal than a few words uttered in a gaming hall."

Arthur stared at him. "You mean—"

"I mean once a duel is fought, and possibly someone killed, every tongue in town will be wagging about the lady who was the cause of it."

Arthur pondered this. "I see. Perhaps it would be better—"

"Yes, it would," said Mr. Carpenter. "Jackson, do you have a pen and paper? Here, Arthur, sit at this table."

By the time the acceptance was delivered and the duel definitely cancelled it was almost dawn. A weary Desmond returned to his quarters and dispatched a servant with a note to Samantha. He smiled thinking of her, as he drifted off to sleep.

She would be so pleased. And so grateful.

CHAPTER FIFTEEN

WHEN HE PRESENTED HIMSELF at Grosvenor Square late the next morning, Desmond was informed by Brooks that his parents were out and that Miss Scarborough was in the library.

He found Samantha, in a crisp morning dress of yellow dimity, seated at a small table by the window. Her head was bent over a note she was penning, and the sun glinted on the bronze curls threaded carelessly with a yellow riband.

He stood for a moment, enjoying the pleasure provided by the sight of her. She was reaching for the sand to blot it, when she saw him.

She rushed to him and took his hand. "Oh, my lord, your missive gave me much relief. It was so kind of you to send it. I was so worried."

"But I told you that all would be well."

"I know you said you would stop it." She gave him an apologetic look. "But Arthur can be so stubborn when he throws himself into one of his roles."

He smiled. "Yes, I know. That was what stopped him."

"Stopped him! I don't understand."

"A hero to the end. When he realized that a duel might be more deadly to his lady love than to himself—"

"How could that be?"

"The wagging tongue of gossip, you know." He shook his head and smiled as he noticed Samantha's telltale dimple appear.

"Oh, that was clever of you. However did you manage to convince him?"

"Never mind that. Just be glad he accepted the note of apology."

"Apology? You got a note of apology from Lord Billington?"

He nodded.

"But however did you manage that? He is so arrogant—so proud!"

"Actually, it was his decision. He seemed convinced that a duel was not the thing."

"You convinced him. I am sure of it. I was just penning a note to Lady Travis suggesting that it might be well to send for Arthur, to keep him out of more scrapes, you know, though of course I didn't say that. But, Mark, it could have been such a different kind of note...." Impulsively she touched his hand. "So kind of you."

Affected by the gesture, Desmond was silent for a moment.

"So kind," Samantha repeated. "And so clever. If it hadn't been for you . . ."

"Oh, come now," he said. "I did nothing."

"Nothing! Nothing! It was not your affair. Yet when I came to you in the middle of the night—" She stopped as if remembering something. She dropped his hand as suddenly as she had seized it and stepped back. "I am so grateful. I can never thank you enough."

Why did she suddenly seem a million miles away? "But you have thanked me," he said. "Quite enough. And now that the episode is over, shall we go for a ride in the park? It's a beautiful day."

"No. That is, I couldn't today. I'm sorry." She actually seemed embarrassed. "I—I promised Lady Marlowe I'd go to Hookham's Library with her this afternoon. Perhaps another time."

"Perhaps," he said coldly. She preferred a visit to the library to a ride with him! "Very well, madam, I bid you good day."

He had reached the door when he heard her call.

"Mark . . ."

He turned. Had she changed her mind?

"Thank you again. I really am very grateful."

"It was nothing," he said once more, and departed.

Samantha swallowed a lump in her throat as she watched him go. Nothing would have pleased her more than a ride in the park with him. But that was just it. She was beginning to be too pleased with his company. She needed time to regain some composure. Last night's wakefulness had not been entirely because of Arthur.

Her imagination had run riot as she tossed and turned on her bed. Dire scenes of a bleeding Arthur were punctuated by a picture of a dashing beauty driving a high-perched phaeton, and over the sounds of clashing swords a seductive voice was heard to ask, "Now who could be visiting you at this hour, my love?"

Samantha sighed.

Well, at least Arthur's dilemma was over. Now she must come to grips with her own. What a silly goose she was, to fall in love with Lord Desmond. In love? No, that was not possible!

It was all a scheme. All pretence. He had told her . . . to protect him from his matchmaking mother. Why hadn't he told her that his heart belonged to another? That he wanted that protection to shield his love from a disapproving mother. Samantha knew the duchess well enough to feel sure that she would never accept that Angel person as Mark's wife.

But how he must love her! To go to such lengths!

Samantha leaned her head against the casement and stared out at the tiny garden. It was neat and orderly. The shrubs were well pruned, the flower beds carefully weeded, the colourful blossoms were bathed in sunlight. It was all so pleasant, so orderly. As if her own world were not shattered and dismal.

"Hearts do not break..." She had read that somewhere. So what was the persistent ache deep inside her? Abruptly she lifted her head.

Samantha Scarborough, you are acting like a lovesick schoolgirl! How could a man break your heart when he never even held it? What a ninny you are!

Theirs had been—still was—a purely business arrangement. And he was certainly living up to his side of the bargain. Emily was having her London come out. No hosts could be more gracious than the duke and duchess. And Desmond was a charming escort. He had played his part and she must play hers.

"Oh, Samantha, there you are." Looking fresh and rested and quite lovely in a gown of flowered muslin, Emily came into the library. "Whatever is the matter with Lord Desmond? He looked so grim and hardly spoke to me when I met him in the hall. Oh, Sam, do you like this dress? Arthur is coming over and I want to look particularly fetching."

"Lovely."

"Oh, Sam, imagine! Arthur didn't have to fight Lord Billington, after all. Isn't that good?"

"A very good thing."

"I was so worried. I declare I didn't sleep a wink last night." Emily adjusted a flounce on her dress and frowned. "I don't know. Maybe I should wear the blue linen. What do you think?"

"You look very nice."

"Well, anyway, I was so overcome at the thought of that dreadful duel that Jenny got the smelling salts and brought me hot milk and everything. Still I couldn't sleep a wink. But I must have dozed off just before dawn, you know, for Jenny had to wake me when she brought my chocolate.

And, oh, Sam there was a note from Arthur saying he didn't have to fight, after all. Lord Billington had apologized. What do you think of that?''

"Amazing."

"Well, I wish I could have seen his face. He must have been frightened out of his wits when Arthur challenged him. Arthur was so angry, you know. He threw a glass of wine in Lord Billington's face and he told him, 'You shall not sully the name of the woman I love.'''

"Yes, Emily, I know."

"Arthur is so chivalrous. He said he only accepted the apology because a duel would cause me further pain. Wasn't it clever of him to think of that."

"Very clever."

"I am persuaded that Arthur is—"

Whatever Emily was to say was cut short by the entrance of Brooks, who presented Samantha with a card.

"Lord Rutherford, ma'am. He is waiting in the front parlour."

"Tell him I cannot—" No, Samantha thought, she should see more of other gentlemen. Anything to distract her thoughts from Lord Desmond. "Tell him I will be right down directly."

"Well," Emily said as she followed Samantha out of the room, "I can still tell Elsie Macon that Arthur almost fought a duel over me. She'll be positively green with jealousy!"

It was not in Samantha's nature to succumb to the blue devils, and though sick at heart, she tried not to do so now. During the following two weeks, she made a valiant effort to keep her part of the bargain. She danced at every rout, was gay and charming at every ball and made morning calls with the duchess. However, she carefully avoided being alone with Desmond, keeping only those engagements which included her grace or Emily and Arthur. He seemed puzzled as well as irked, and several times attempted to ascertain what was amiss. She smiled brightly, declared that everything was fine and continued to evade him as much as possible.

Samantha was determined to turn her thoughts away from Desmond, and she was not without the power to do so. Several gentlemen had become attracted to the "Scarborough girl with the copper curls," and left their calling cards at Grosvenor Square with invitations for every conceivable amusement. Lord Jason Rutherford was the most persistent of these suitors. Several times each week, he brought his Miss Silver over and took Samantha out for an early morning canter.

It was after one of these rides that Lord Rutherford followed Samantha into the small salon. He stood for a moment fingering his riding gloves, then spoke very softly. "Miss Scarborough, have I your permission to speak with your uncle?"

Samantha looked her surprise. "My permission? Why? You are good friends and Uncle Stanley is most approachable, the very best of good fellows—" She broke off as she realized his meaning.

He laughed. "My dear girl, that is what I like about you. So innocent, so artless. Did you not guess that you had captured my heart?"

"Oh, please, sir. Say no more."

It was as if he had not heard her. "And when I talked with you I knew you were the only woman in the world for me. There was none of that frippery nonsensical chatter one is accustomed to hearing from your sex. You and I spoke only of horses. And you advised me to buy Timberlake."

"But I didn't advise you!"

"Not precisely. But what you said convinced me! Your interest, or perhaps the expertise you display in that field. I share that interest, my dear. Oh, such a pair we will make!"

"I pray, sir, do consider." Surely he couldn't think a mutual interest in horses a sound basis for marriage! "Lord Rutherford, you mistake—"

"Yes, my darling, from the first moment I saw you in the ballroom, with your hair glowing in the candlelight and that green dress swirling about you. You looked like some beautiful wood nymph."

"Lord, Rutherford, please. You mistake—"

"Mistake? No, indeed, dear girl. No one could mistake your interest in that quarter. When they brought out your Black Knight... Such a beautiful beast. He will make history. I could see that."

Samantha held up a protesting hand. "You do not understand. I—"

"Of course I understand. I, too, am an excellent judge of horses. You have not seen my stable. Miss Silver, she is nothing. Why, at my yearly hunt party..." His voice softened. "Ah, I can see you now, seated on Dancing Dolly, leading the chase. A beautiful lady on a beautiful beast. The Countess of Sussex."

"Lord Rutherford, you do me a great honour, but..."

"No, my darling, it is I who will be honoured." He seized both her hands and kissed them passionately. "Just tell me, my sweet, that I may speak with your uncle."

"I beg your pardon. Do I intrude?"

Samantha pulled her hands away and stepped back to face Lord Desmond. He stood in the doorway, eyes blazing, his face grim and unsmiling.

CHAPTER SIXTEEN

SAMANTHA FELT her face burn. "Of course you do not intrude," she said. "Lord Rutherford was just taking his leave."

Rutherford's eyes darted from Samantha to Desmond, and back to Samantha. "Precisely," he said, bowing low before her. "Until tomorrow, my love." Retrieving his gloves from the table, he gave Desmond a curt nod and walked out.

Desmond frowned at Samantha. "What is the meaning of that?"

"I suppose he means that he will return sometime tomorrow," Samantha answered, trying to speak calmly, though rather startled by his tone.

"'My love'!" Desmond's face was livid.

"Ju-just an expression," she stammered.

"And the way he was kissing your hands! I suppose that was just an expression, too!"

Vexed by his proprietary manner, she spoke sharply. "In any case, sir, that is no concern of yours."

"No concern of mine, eh? Egad! You are supposed to be engaged to me!"

"You mistake, sir," Samantha answered quietly. "The situation is that you are thinking of offering for me."

"Don't mince words, my girl!" Desmond clapped a hand to the back of his neck in exasperation. "The fact is that you are a guest in my parents' home on the pretext of an intimate relationship with me. How do you suppose it looks to my mother—and yes, to her friends—when you are flirting with every jackanapes who darkens our door?''

''Flirting! You are accusing me of flirting?''

''Perhaps I should say...what was the term you used? Oh, yes, casting out lures!''

''Need you insult me, my lord?''

''Oh, Samantha, pray forgive me,'' he said quickly. ''I didn't mean that. It's just that you provoke me beyond reason. I scarcely realize what I am saying.''

''You seem easily provoked, my lord. I was merely entertaining a morning caller.''

''On rather intimate terms I apprehend. And really, Sam, it passes my comprehension that you find the time to entertain any gentleman who leaves his calling card except me!''

''I fail to see why it should pass your comprehension when it was your suggestion.''

''My suggestion?''

''Certainly. I seem to recall a conversation in which you indicated...let's see, how did you put it? Something about my choosing from the many suitors who might offer for me. Wasn't that it?''

Desmond tugged at his neckcloth. ''I did not mean that suitor!''

''I was not under the impression that you were to make the choice.''

''Am I to understand that you have made a choice?''

Samantha fingered the edge of her handkerchief. ''Lord Rutherford seems to be a person of estimable character.''

''Jason Rutherford is a scoundrel who provides a choice mare for your morning canters, while Hookham's library is more preferable than a morning canter with me!''

''The early morning hours, remember? In London, you are hardly abroad before noon.''

''As your betrothed, your rides would be more properly taken with me, my dear girl!''

"Your betrothed?" Samantha threw up her hands. "When does this farce end, my lord?"

"At the altar, if need be."

Samantha stared at him in shocked surprise. "You go to a great deal of trouble, my lord, to conceal your real desires."

"What do you mean by that?"

Feeling her eyes well with tears, she turned away from him. He reached out, cupped her chin and turned her face back to him. "What is it, Samantha? Are you angry with me?"

"Of course not!"

"Then what has happened? What has come between us?"

"Nothing." He was looking at her with those caressing eyes, and it was all she could do to hold back the tears.

"You are avoiding me!"

"I am not. It is just that... that I don't like this deception."

"And why not, my dear? I am rather enjoying it."

"How could you! When you... when..." But she couldn't say it, couldn't utter the words. She was just a camouflage for the woman he really loved, and she couldn't bear it.

"Samantha, wait!" she heard him call. But already she was running up the stairs.

LORD RUTHERFORD managed to leave Duval House calmly, but deep inside he was seething, hardly knowing who was the greater target of his anger—Samantha or Desmond. He had the distinct impression that she had been about to refuse his offer of marriage.

I am Jason Rutherford, earl of Sussex, the most sought after bachelor in the whole of the realm. Samantha Scarborough was the only woman to whom he had ever offered his hand in marriage. And she, after dallying with him for weeks, had the audacity to spurn that offer! Oh, yes, he had a score to settle with that saucy miss!

And he had an older score to settle with Desmond. Somehow that gentleman always managed to best him, no matter what game they played. And this morning he had seen that murderous look in Desmond's eyes. He had departed, having no wish that Rutherford blood be spilled on her grace's pretty carpet. But this game is not yet over, he promised himself.

At home, Lord Rutherford sat in his library and thoughtfully sipped his brandy. Desmond had the look of a man in love. Did Samantha know? No, he reasoned, she did not. Unless, of course, the fool was confessing to her now.

Lord Rutherford looked hard at his brandy, turning the glass round and round. He made a habit of studying the nature of his adversaries, and he thought he knew Lord Desmond well. Desmond was a man determined not to be caught in the matrimonial trap, and, though at home with the muslin set, had spent his life avoiding entanglements with ladies of quality. Habits were hard to break, and as yet no banns had been posted.

Suddenly the earl stood, hot blood rushing to his face as he was seized by an idea. Had the lady been using him, dallying with him for weeks to bring Lord Desmond to the point? Or was she now holding him at bay until she could divine the other man's intention? For this morning, she had not precisely given him an answer, and she had seemed glad when they were interrupted by Desmond. Possibly she hoped to goad that gentleman into such a jealous rage that he would declare himself!

Indeed, he had noticed several times the way she looked at Desmond. He felt she would go running if Desmond lifted one finger—that is, if the finger held a ring. Miss Samantha Scarborough was a very proper lady.

Proper. By Jove, that was it! He sent for Clarence, his groom. Then, chuckling to himself, he sat down to write a note. If his plan worked, Miss Scarborough would be willing—even begging—to marry him.

And whether he married her or not, he would wreak his vengeance upon them both!

CHAPTER SEVENTEEN

RUTHERFORD'S NOTE delivered to Samantha that evening, informed her that tomorrow afternoon would be a good time to visit the museum to see the Grecian marbles, as a lecturer explaining them would be present then. Would it be convenient for him to call for her at one the next day?

Still smarting from her recent encounter with Desmond, Samantha sent a reply that she would be delighted. She had a double reason for accepting the invitation. She really did want to see the marbles and she had to make Lord Rutherford understand that she was refusing his offer of marriage. Desmond's interruption had given her no opportunity to do so yesterday.

Precisely at one the following day, Samantha was handed into Lord Rutherford's curricle. She was fetchingly clad in an apricot muslin walking dress which had a tight-fitting bodice and was flounced at the hem. She carried a matching parasol with deep ruffles.

Jason Rutherford's eyes lit up at the sight of her. "Stunning! You look like a bride," he whispered, his voice full of meaning.

Samantha retained her smile, but something in his tone irked her. An implication, as if... Oh, good heavens! Had he misunderstood her refusal yesterday? Then she felt her cheeks burn as she remembered how they had been interrupted. Well, she must not allow him to be under a misapprehension. "Lord Rutherford," she began, "yesterday—"

"Was far more dismal than today," he said as he took the reins. "We are indeed fortunate that we have the sun, for the lecture is scheduled in the garden of the museum."

Samantha watched him turn the horses about. She was surprised to see him driving his own curricle, and without a groom behind. Never had she seen him without his faithful Clarence. She glanced uneasily at him.

Although he was reputed to be an expert horseman, she didn't like the way Lord Rutherford handled his horses. His whip cracked frequently and his hands were tight on the reins. He was so different from Desmond. Desmond held the reins loosely, letting the horses have their head, almost as if they were guiding themselves. Strange, how you could read a man's character by the way he handled his horses.

These two men were as different as night and day. For all his perfect manners, she sensed cruelty in Lord Rutherford. Desmond was kind, gentle. That first day, after he had released Haro, her treasured spaniel, from the trap, he had handled him so gently, had spoken in such soothing tones. Watching Desmond astride Black Knight, she had known that for all his gentleness, he was the master. Strong and gentle, different and wonderful qualities.

Thinking of Desmond, her mind flew to the previous day—their last stormy encounter. There had been nothing gentle about Desmond when he had come upon her and Lord Rutherford. He had been exceedingly rude, and gruff, almost as if he were in a jealous rage! But of course that could not be, and she felt her anger flare up again. He was a demanding proprietary man! How dared he act as if he owned her! He had no right to tell her whom she should or should not see. He carried the farce too far! Too far, indeed! What was it he had said about it ending at the altar, if need be?

She felt her cheeks grow hot as she remembered how he had turned her toward him, her chin in his hand. His fingers had burnt into her skin, and she felt her eyes smart as she struggled to hide her feelings.

Samantha sat up with a start. Dear heavens! It was she who was jealous. Mad with jealousy over a raven-haired beauty who held his heart! And she had no right! No right at all!

He had asked if she had been avoiding him. Yes, she had been. She had not been fair. He had tried to be a friend, and she had been acting as if he had betrayed her. That wasn't fair. So deep had she been in her thoughts of Desmond that she had not noted the route Rutherford travelled. Now she looked to find that they were no longer among houses and shops, but were on a road she didn't recognize.

She turned to Lord Rutherford. "This isn't the way to the museum! I was under the impression that it was near Tottenham Court Road."

His eyes darted toward her and away. "I think you will like where I am taking you, my dear."

"But the museum—the marbles... Where are you taking me?"

"A surprise, dear lady, which will far surpass the Grecian marbles."

Again she felt that little prickle of fear. She forced herself to speak calmly. "I do not like surprises."

His lips parted in imitation of a smile. "I think you will like this one. Have you ever been to Scotland?"

"No."

"I think you will like Gretna Greene. Such a quaint town."

"Perhaps... if I should ever visit there." She tried to laugh. Surely he was teasing her. "Lord Rutherford, do turn back. We shall be late for the lecture."

"But I told you. We are not going to the lecture. We are going to Gretna Greene."

"Please, sir, do be serious. Let us turn back."

"But, my dear, I am serious." He took one hand from the reins and placed it over hers. "I decided to take your advice, my darling, at Gretna Greene."

"My advice? Gretna Greene? Why, I never suggested such a thing!" His touch was clammy, she drew her hand away and looked at him incredulously. "How could you think such a thing?"

The beady eyes bulged in pretended surprise. "You said there was no need to speak to your uncle."

"Of course there was no need to speak to my uncle, for I had no intention— Forgive me, sir, but this is the time for plain speaking. I have no intention of marrying you."

"Well, you certainly led me to believe otherwise. Indeed, you gave me every encouragement, receiving my attentions graciously, I might say even eagerly. I had every reason to believe that you returned my affections."

"But surely you could not think that—" She faltered. Had she, in her zeal to turn away from Desmond been, as he suggested, *casting out lures*? "Surely, sir, a few rides on your Miss Silver could not be interpreted as—as a wish to marry you."

"But yesterday you said you were honoured."

"Oh, sir, you mistook my meaning. We were interrupted and I had no chance to give you a proper answer."

"That is unfortunate."

"Yes, of course, and I am sorry. But now that you understand..." She looked around. The horses were going at a much faster rate. "Please, sir, we should turn back immediately."

"I'm afraid it's too late for that." His eyes were on the fast-moving horses and he did not look at her.

"Too late!" she echoed. "Surely you can not mean to travel all the way to Gretna Greene like this." With a wave of her hand she indicated the open carriage.

Now he did look at her, and there was a triumphant gleam in his eyes. "Of course not. My travelling coach will be waiting at The Iron Horse, equipped with every necessity for a long journey.''

This was no misunderstanding. This had been carefully planned.

Samantha drew herself up, more angry than afraid. ''My good sir, had I accepted your proposal, which I certainly did not, even then I would not consent to flee in this disgraceful fashion. My uncle will—''

''Your uncle, I am persuaded, will be pleased. His affairs are in such disorder that . . . well, suffice it to say that I am a very wealthy man.''

''That does not signify! This is preposterous! You cannot force me to marry you.''

He shrugged. ''Of course not. The choice shall be yours. But after two nights spent alone with me as we travel to Scotland, you might consider carefully the alternatives.''

''This is unbelievable. Abominable! You are a beast!''

''On the contrary, my dear. I am not a mean man. As Lady Rutherford, I promise you you will lack for nothing.''

Samantha felt dizzy. She clutched the handrail to steady herself. Her mind reeled, but on one point it was clear. She would *never* become Lady Rutherford. This was ridiculous. He could not force her into submission. When they reached The Iron Horse, she would appeal for help, solicit a ride back to London.

Lord Rutherford spoke, his voice soft and mocking. ''I think you will find The Iron Horse quite comfortable, my dear. The owner is an old friend of mine. In fact, he is indebted to me and very eager to please.

CHAPTER EIGHTEEN

LORD DESMOND FROWNED as he sat at his desk. Lately he had been puzzled by Samantha's cool treatment of himself. Now he was incensed!

Had Rutherford brought about the change in her attitude? Had that cad managed to worm his way into her affections with his perfect manners and his prize mare and his pretentious chatter about his stable and his estate? Oh, women were always agog over titles and wealth!

But, no. Not Samantha. If she loved a man she wouldn't care a fig about his estate. She had said, "Lord Rutherford seems a person of estimable character."

The marquis slammed his hand on his desk and stood.

Ha! What do you know, my lady! You've never watched him deal from the bottom of the deck. Nor have you seen that scowl on his face when he is bested. Such a man will not have you. I'll see to that!

"I was not under the impression that you were to make the choice"

We'll see about that, madam! You're in London under my protection, in a manner of speaking, and I'll see to it that you make mo misalliance with that cur.

He had been pacing the floor in rage, but now he stopped, struck by the firm conviction that he would do all in his power to prevent her marriage with any man but himself. Because he damme well could not live without her!

Didn't she know that? Didn't she know how much he loved her?

You didn't know it yourself, you fool! Samantha had crept so silently into his heart, so quickly and easily had she become the centre of his whole life, that he hadn't realized it was love. And by the time he did, she had changed. Ever since the night she had come to him about the duel.

And since that night ... What had happened? Why had Samantha turned away from him? They had been dealing so well together, and he had begun to think she also cared for him. What had happened?

He was determined to get some understanding from her. Twice that evening he called at Grosvenor Square, but each time she remained closeted in her room, and he had no chance of an audience with her.

He did, however, have an audience with his father, who had requested Mark to travel to Somerset the next day to transact some pressing business for him.

"Yes," Mark promised. "I will go, as soon as ..." He hesitated, glancing at the duke. "That is, immediately after I've talked with Samantha."

His grace raised an eyebrow, but only said in his noncommittal way, "Very well."

It was in preparation for his journey to Somerset that the marquis came upon a strange bit of news in a most unusual way. He had instructed Clinton to get everything in readiness. Remembering a broken spoke on one of the wheels of the travelling coach, Clinton had accordingly taken that vehicle to the wheelwright to be repaired. He returned on horseback to pack his master's gear and to inform Jiggs, the coachman, to be ready to leave that afternoon, whereupon he was berated by Jiggs for usurping his duties. It was his place to take the coach in for repair, and he would certainly have remembered that the brakes were loose and so informed the wheelwright. When Desmond happened in upon the tongue-lashing, there was some disagreement as to whose duty it was to return to town to convey this message to the wheelwright.

Desmond solved the problem. He would undertake this duty, as he was going that way on a personal errand. Desmond's business, before seeing Samantha, was in Bond Street. Passing a window late last evening, he had caught sight of a diamond tiara. Not as elaborate as his mother's, but dainty and delicate, scattered with diamonds. How they would sparkle in Samantha's hair! She should be pleased. If he knew anything about women, he knew they liked expensive trinkets. But . . . he stirred uneasily in his saddle, instinctively knowing that Samantha cared as little about such trinkets as she did about titles.

Still, he hoped she would be pleased, and pictured in his mind her sweet forgiving smile. For later last evening, when he could think more rationally, he realized how in his fury he had lashed out at her. His manner had been unpardonable, and she had a right to be angry. He wanted to take her in his arms, beg her forgiveness and make her know how much he loved her.

At the jeweller's, he studied the tiara, considering whether to add an emerald. It would catch the green of her eyes. But, no. He liked the elegant simplicity of the plain diamonds. It was quietly elegant, like Samantha herself.

With the gift in his pocket and an apology forming on his lips, he rode toward Grosvenor Square. She must know that he did not mean what he had said. He had quite forgot about his promised message about the brake. But the sight of Jake, the wheelwright, repairing a spoke on his own travelling coach, reminded him.

He told Jake about the problem, then, looking about the crowded shop, commented, "Busy day today, eh?"

"Right about that, your lordship. Seems like everybody's in a rush today. Mr. Darcy lost a wheel, and before I could get to that, here's both you and Lord

Rutherford wanting your travelling coaches looked after, and right now. I expect you're both off to Doncaster.''

Desmond smiled and then nodded to Clarence, Lord Rutherford's groom, who had turned from saddling his horses. ''Not I. Have to miss the races. I'm off to Somerset.''

As he turned to mount his horse, he heard Clarence say to Jake, ''We ain't going to the races, neither. And me with a tip on the neatest little mare you ever seen—Miss Starlight in the third heat.''

''Ain't like Lord Rutherford to miss the races,'' Jake commented.

''Well, he's missing this one,'' was Clarence's answer. ''I'm to call for him at The Iron Horse. Did you check that axle?''

What in the world did Rutherford want at The Iron Horse? Was he travelling north? Well, it didn't matter. At least he would be out of Samantha's pocket for a while.

Desmond rode on to Grosvenor Square, where he was informed by Brooks that Miss Scarborough was out attending a lecture at the museum with Lord Rutherford.

How could Lord Rutherford be on his way to Scotland and attending a lecture with Samantha at the same time? Desmond stood on the steps, pondering.

SHE WAS BEING ABDUCTED! That one unbelievable but inescapable fact loomed in Samantha's mind as she held on tight to the handrail and watched the galloping horses. She did not scream, for who was to hear her? And this was not the time to succumb to a fit of the vapours. Wildly she considered some means of escape. She could not jump from the carriage, for if she did not break a leg or, worse still, her neck, where would she go? Lord Rutherford had made it clear there would be no help at The Iron Horse. Did he plan to stay there for the night? Perhaps at the next posting station when they stopped to change horses, she could slip away.

Why had she worn this stupid hat that tied under her chin? Another kind would have had a hat pin. One quick jab and a hefty push and she could drive herself back to London. She looked at her captor and contemplated. Would a hefty push without the jab unseat him? If she took him by surprise?

He had slowed their pace now and kept glancing over his shoulder. Samantha looked back and saw someone on horseback far in the distance. Some farmer, perhaps. She would call to him if he did not turn off and if he caught up with them. Lord Rutherford had slackened speed, probably not wanting to attract attention. The rider was gaining on them.

Rutherford gave one long look at the approaching rider, then turned suddenly, urging the horses on, faster and faster. He was driving like a demon now, head bent, lashing wildly with his whip. Samantha could not look back. She was clinging desperately to the handrail, afraid that the carriage would overturn. She could hear the hoofbeats behind them coming closer and closer. Ahead she saw a narrow bridge and wondered if the horses could make it at this rapid pace.

Before they reached the bridge, the rider was beside them. He was blocked from her view by the bulky form of Rutherford, but she tried to call out to him. Her voice was drowned by the clatter of hooves and the rider swept by. Hope died within her when she heard the iron shoes of the horse thud against the wooden planks of the bridge as the rider sped across and disappeared from sight around a bend in the road.

In evident relief, Rutherford pulled back on the reins, again slowing their pace, and they crossed safely. Then Samantha was almost propelled from her seat as the carriage made a turn, lurched suddenly to the right and abruptly stopped. Their way was blocked by the horse and rider.

"Desmond! You dog!" Rutherford shouted, trying to control the neighing horses.

It was Desmond! Samantha felt an overwhelming sense of relief. He was here. He would take care of her. She was safe.

Desmond leapt swiftly from his saddle to the carriage, seized Lord Rutherford's neckcloth and pulled him to the ground. Both men rolled in the dust. At first Samantha feared for Desmond as Rutherford was the stockier of the two. But Desmond fought as one possessed, his fury seeming to mount as he thrashed Rutherford, knocking him to the ground again and again. Soon Samantha saw that Rutherford's nose was bleeding, his eye was cut, and his breath came in short gasps. Unheeding, Desmond continued to pummel him mercilessly.

"Oh, stop! Do stop!" she shouted, afraid that Desmond might actually kill him. She jumped down from the carriage and rushed toward them.

Desmond gave Lord Rutherford one last punch, which sent him reeling backward. Rutherford hit the earth with a thud, rolled down the bank toward the stream and lay quite still.

"Oh, my God!" Samantha breathed. Was he dead? Oh, no! That couldn't be. Mark would be a murderer.

She ran to the stream, dripped her handkerchief in the water and dabbed at Lord Rutherford's face. She was relieved to see him open one eye as he struggled to rise.

"Oh, thank goodness," she gasped. "I thought—"

Before she could finish her sentence, she felt herself roughly seized, thrown over Desmond's shoulder and dumped unceremoniously into the carriage. He said nothing, but tied his horse behind the carriage, got into the driver's seat and turned the vehicle toward London.

Samantha saw Lord Rutherford climbing up the bank and calling to them. Seeing him very much alive, she could give vent to her feelings. Served him right! Let him walk back to town or to that Iron Horse, where his very good friends were!

Desmond paid no heed to her, but drove on, his face set. His clothes were rumpled and dusty and there was a small cut on one cheek.

A wave of tenderness swept over Samantha. She wanted to tend the cut, to brush back that lock of hair falling over his left eye, to caress his cheek and kiss away the hurt. She felt her own cheeks grow hot and flushed. Of course she couldn't do that. His love belonged to someone else.

Still, he had saved her! A little rough, perhaps, but he had saved her! She turned toward him, a grateful smile on her face.

The glance he returned cut like a whip, and there was a restrained bitterness in his voice. "I apprehend quite clearly your anxiety to escape my protection and confirm your alliance with Lord Rutherford, but I assure you I will not let it happen."

Stunned with surprise, Samantha opened her mouth, but no words came.

"Especially," he continued, "when you are living in my parents' home and under my protection. That you could allow your emotions for that scoundrel to overcome your respect for the proper mode of behaviour is reprehensible."

"Oh, you wrong me," she cried. "I never—"

"Forgive me. Perhaps I underrate your great *love*." He turned toward her, and she shrank from the wild fury in his eyes. "But how that love could be bestowed on a weasel like Jason Rutherford is beyond me."

"You don't understand. I was so frightened."

"There was no need to be. I had no intention of killing him. My intention was to prevent you from bringing disgrace upon my father's house."

"Me? Disgrace?"

"Perhaps you have resided too long and too isolated in the country to be aware of the scandal which would be created by an elopement to Gretna Green. But no matter how strong your feelings are toward Rutherford, I certainly will not allow such an alliance. Really, Sam, to steal away from my parents' home in such a manner."

Samantha felt a sharp pain in her right hand. Looking down, she loosened the tight grip on her parasol. She struggled to keep her voice calm and even. "Lord Desmond, are you under the impression that I was willingly accompanying Lord Rutherford?"

"*Accompanying* him?" His laugh was harsh and grating. "Hardly. I think the term is *seduction*."

"You are accusing me—"

"Of using your womanly wiles to induce him to do just as you wished. Probably making your plans when I interrupted you yesterday. I see that my warning did nothing to dissuade you."

Infuriated beyond speech by his stinging accusations, Samantha stared fixedly at her parasol, angrily considering that, in place of a hat pin, it could have been used as a weapon against her captor. Now she felt a burning desire to thwack it repeatedly across the head of her rescuer.

"Have you nothing to say for yourself?" that gentleman asked, an almost plaintive note in his voice. "No shame? No apology?"

"Nothing." Let him think what he pleased.

"I must say I did not expect it of you. I should have, of course. I am well acquainted with all the female tricks."

"That much is certainly true."

He shot her a suspicious glance, hesitated, then continued in the same vein. "I repeat, it matters little to me who falls victim to your seductive charms. But I tell you plainly, as long as you are residing at Grosvenor Square, I shall not tolerate this unseemly behaviour.''

''You will not tolerate it?''

''Certainly not. There has never been a breath of scandal in my father's home!''

''That, undoubtedly, is due to the fact that *you* are not living there.''

''You are!'' he retorted. ''And as long as you are, I will make it my duty to see that your affairs are honourably conducted.''

She gave him an icy smile. ''I do appreciate your concern. And I shall soon relieve you of that responsibility, for I shall rid you of my company this very evening.''

''Indeed you will not.''

She stared at him, amazed. ''Surely you cannot expect me to remain after this.''

''Indeed I do expect you to remain. I have to go to Somerset for a few days, and I only hope that you will act with decorum while I'm away. We made a bargain, you and I. The circumstances have not altered. It is your conduct which is in question.''

''My conduct!'' Samantha, goaded beyond endurance, spoke crisply. ''You seem to have a pretty habit, my lord, of calling the kettle black.''

''And just what do you mean by that?''

''I mean that you should first take heed of the mote in your own eye before passing judgement upon me! When an unmarried man entertains a woman at odd hours in his private quarters, I should think that it is his conduct which is in question.''

He gave her an odd look in which there was a flicker of understanding. ''Is that it? You knew? That night, when you came to me, you... Were you under the impression that I was entertaining... that someone... a woman was present?''

"There was no mistaking that feminine voice—" She stopped. Samantha choked back a sob and was glad to note that they were now turning on the cobbled street that led to Grosvenor Square. Soon she could go to her own room and hide her hurt.

"The circumstances were not as you imagine. Let me explain."

"I assure you that an explanation is unnecessary. Your reputation is well-known to me. And, although I cannot understand the arbiters of society who wink at such behaviour in a gentleman, and yet are scandalized by an elopement with marriage in mind, which seems to me vastly more respectable, I do concede your right to live as you choose."

"Your conduct, dear lady, was reprehensible. And you are under a misapprehension concerning mine."

"Nevertheless, I beg you, do not speak to me of decorum until you are no longer hiding the woman you love behind a pretext of affection for me!"

"Hiding?" He had stopped before Duval House and was staring at her in amazement. "The woman I love? Do you mean . . . Angel?"

"Yes. I believe that is the name I heard." She did not wait for him to help her, but jumped lightly down and ran up the steps of the house.

He quickly followed. "Samantha, I cannot allow you to remain under a false impression concerning my attachment."

Having vigorously applied the knocker, she now turned to face him. "Your attachments, sir, are of no concern to me. Still, it might be well for you to contrive an elopement to Gretna Green yourself. Then you would be able to present your beloved to society in the respectable guise of your wife!"

Desmond started to speak, but the footman had opened the door, and Samantha brushed past him and rushed to the safety of her room.

Alone at last, she threw aside her hat and parasol, and flung herself face down on the bed. At last she could give full vent to the feelings of anger, frustration and hurt that were seething within her. She was utterly ashamed. Crying was a sign of weakness and tears never solved anything.

But how could he think such a thing of her? Not that what he thought mattered. She hated him!

CHAPTER NINETEEN

ALWAYS ADEPT at hiding her feelings, Samantha managed to conceal her inner turmoil from her hosts. Outwardly she was calm and cheerful and went about as usual, honouring each invitation she had accepted. She did, however, inform Brooks that she was not at home to any casual gentleman caller. Several left their cards, but there was none from Lord Jason Rutherford.

Later that week, at an afternoon tea, she overheard a conversation that revealed Lord Rutherford was on an extended tour of the Continent. Samantha smiled to herself. Of course. He would not dare expose his bruised face to a curious ton.

Samantha's feelings concerning the absent Desmond vacillated. One moment she longed to see him, to explain away the bitterness between them. The next moment she vowed never to meet him again and made plans to leave London before his return. Samantha felt no qualms about leaving. Desmond's unjust accusations invalidated any agreement they had made. But how was she to explain her sudden departure to his parents? And to Emily, reunited with Arthur, and all agog about their forthcoming nuptials? Each day Samantha pondered this dilemma and frantically searched for any excuse to return to Scarborough. The excuse came unexpectedly, plunging Samantha deep into another kind of trouble.

"Lord Scarborough, my lady."

"Thank you, Brooks." She would be glad to see Uncle Stanley, but sorry to admit that she had not yet seen Lady Atterley.

In the drawing room, Lord Scarborough stood and stared out of the window. He looked a little thinner. Had he, Samantha wondered, been using one of Lord Byron's reducing remedies? Or perhaps this business about Matilda had him so downcast that he wasn't eating properly.

"Oh, Uncle," she greeted him. "I haven't yet been able to see Lady Atterley. They are out of town."

He turned toward her with such a worried look that she felt a stab of apprehension. She had never seen him this perturbed, even when he had informed her of his betrothal.

"What is it, Uncle? Has something else happened?"

"Nothing, child, nothing." He took her hand and patted it absentmindedly. "It's just that I, er, well, I've got to go away for a while. I thought that—that is, it's necessary that I get you safely back to Scarborough before I go."

"Of course," Samantha said, relieved at the prospect.

"I'm sorry, Sam. I hate to interrupt your visit."

"Oh, no," she cried. "I'm longing to go home."

"Are you now?" His surprise was evident. "I had thought you and Desmond... Now, Sam, don't look so upset. I thought you had reached an understanding. But if that ain't the case it's all the more imperative that I see you settled in Scarborough before I go away."

"Of course. When shall we be ready?"

"Tomorrow. It's important that we depart as soon as possible. I want to get back there and make ready to, er, to leave."

"When will you leave, Uncle, and where are you going?" She had an impression that he might have decided to flee the country to escape the impending marriage, and wondered if such a drastic step was necessary.

"I, er, that is, I am not sure." He took a snuff box from his pocket, fumbled with it a moment, forgetting to take snuff, then put it back in his pocket. "I—my plans are uncertain."

Somewhere deep in Samantha's brain, a warning bell sounded, triggered by a memory.

Something Lord Rutherford had said.

"Your uncle . . . his affairs are in such disorder."

"Uncle Stanley, are you in trouble?"

"Why, no, of course not. Whatever gave you such an idea?"

"Your uncle will be pleased. I am a very wealthy man."

"Financial trouble, Uncle Stanley?"

He gave her such a startled look that she knew she was right.

"Your debts?" she inquired. "Are they going to put you in that horrible place Simmons calls the sponging house?"

"Now, now, child. Don't fret. It's not such a horrible place. They say once you've become accustomed to the routine, you—"

"And you weren't even going to tell me!"

"Now, now. I don't want to bother you with my troubles."

"Your troubles! When you had two selfish greedy girls hanging on your sleeve!" Oh, how could she? Simmons had warned her and she had not heeded. She had let Uncle Stanley buy all those clothes and gone gadding about London absorbed in nothing but her own pleasure. "It's all my fault," she whispered.

"Nonsense, child. Fact is, you brought me a bit of luck. Remember Ascot? Thing is, I didn't have you with me at Doncaster. Sorriest bunch of nags you ever saw. Fairly cleaned me out. Ain't done too well with the ivories, either."

"My fault," she insisted. "Making you come to town and spend all that money. And getting betrothed besides."

He gave a start. "Betrothed? By Gad, that's right. I forgot."

"And I'm sorry I haven't been able to see Lady Atterley."

But he had brightened somewhat. "Well, that's a devilish good thing. Now I've got a good reason to cry off. Not good ton!"

"What's not good ton?"

"To be connected with a man who's going to prison. Well that's a good thing. I can just dash off a note to Lady Atterley, and—"

"Oh, Uncle," Samantha gave an indulgent shake of her head. "A good thing to cry off, maybe, but not a good thing for you to go to prison."

"Turn of the luck, Sam. The rule is play or pay. Now it's my turn to pay."

"No, no." Samantha flung her arms around him in a protective grip. She could not bear it. She could not stand to see this careless, carefree, lovable uncle shut away from the world he loved. "It will not happen. We will do something."

"There, there, child," he soothed.

"We'll sell Scarborough!"

"Sell the roof from over you? As if I would! Even if I could. Entailed, you know."

"Well, then, the horses."

"All gone," he confessed. Then, at her shocked look, he added, "Not Black Knight. He's yours. Couldn't sell him. Good thing, too. He's so famous now his stud fees will keep you in pin money for the rest of your life."

It came to her then. Black Knight! The Newmarket Classic. But did they have time?

"How long, Uncle?"

"They've given me a month to clear up my affairs. That's why I want to take you to Scarborough and—"

"Then we do have time."

"What's on your mind, Puss?"

"We'll enter Black Knight in the Newmarket Classic. He'll win. You know he'll win."

"Well, I don't think the Gold Cup will pay off my creditors."

"But if we were to place a big bet on him?"

His eyes twinkled. "You gambling?" Then he shook his head ruefully. "It would take a mighty hefty stake, and I ain't got a feather. Even if I did, there's a debt of honour—had to give a fellow my note."

Samantha's eyes flashed. "Pooh on your debts of honour. Whatever we have we'll place on Black Knight. And whatever we win will be used to pay your creditors, not your gambling debts."

Lord Scarborough smiled. "Well, it don't matter. Can't post a bet without the ready."

But Samantha was busy making plans. Aunt Agatha's jewels! She had never liked the heavy cumbersome things, anyway. But if they could double or even triple their value, for Black Knight was sure to win. She had a little trouble convincing Uncle Stanley, but in the end his gambling spirit was aroused.

One thing, though, he insisted on. No need to tell Lady Atterley there was a possibility he might escape the prison gates, for if she thought he was on his way to the sponging house...

Samantha laughingly agreed that yes, a note to Lady Atterley was in order. He had an excellent excuse to cry off. Lord Scarborough went to pawn the jewels, and Samantha made ready to leave the following day.

It was not an easy leave-taking. The duke and duchess seemed genuinely sorry to see them go. His grace exclaimed that he was losing his best opponent at the chessboard, and the duchess, with a significant glance at Samantha, declared they should at least wait until Mark returned. Emily complained bitterly that it was too cruel to remove just at the height of the season, and Arthur wanted particularly to speak with Uncle Stanley. She knew he would give his consent, of course, and it would be the best of all things for her to buy her bride clothes while they were still in London and not to have to make a return trip.

Samantha was not to be deterred. She thanked their hosts and bade them a fond farewell. By noon, their equipage was loaded and the three Scarboroughs were off for home.

WHEN DESMOND RETURNED a few days later, he stopped at his quarters only long enough to change and went immediately to Grosvenor Square, telling himself that the business with his father must be hastily concluded.

But it was not of business that he spoke when he faced his father in the library. "Brooks tells me that Samantha is gone."

"Samantha?" His father looked up from the table. "Oh. That's right. You didn't know? She left several days ago."

"Rutherford!" Desmond's hand clenched on his riding crop. By God, he might have to kill him, after all!

"Jason Rutherford?" The duke paused in the act of opening his tobacco tin. "A pompous ass. And I make the comparison advisedly, with apologies to the poor donkey. But what has he to do with Samantha?"

"I believe she has a tendre for him."

"And you thought...?" His grace's hearty laughter rang out. "No, Samantha left with her uncle for Scarborough."

"Oh."

Calmly stuffing his pipe with tobacco, the duke gave him a keen look. "I infer that your vast experience has taught you nothing."

"Nothing?"

"About women."

"About women?"

"If you think a woman like Samantha could be attracted to a coxcomb like Jason Rutherford, you still have much to learn." He pointed his pipe stem accusingly at his son. "You've been too long among the muslin set."

Desmond stared at his father. Could he have been wrong? His cravat felt tight and he loosened it.

"Too long gathering rosebuds," his father continued.

"Rosebuds?" At a motion from the duke, he laid aside his hat and riding crop, lighted a splint from the fire and held it to the duke's pipe.

The duke drew on his pipe several times, then, settling back in his chair, mused, "How did that poet fellow put it? 'Gather ye rosebuds while ye may,' and then, 'while ye may, go marry.'"

"You begin to sound much like my mother."

"Oh, no, not at all," the duke said with a chuckle. "It just occurs to me that you've been doing a powerful lot of thinking lately, and while you're thinking, others..." He paused, taking a long draw on his pipe. "Well, suffice it to say, Lord Rutherford is not the only gentleman who has been wearing out my door knocker. Samantha is an exceptional girl."

"I know that." Desmond gave a fire log an impatient kick with his boot.

"Oh, then you know this. An exceptional girl, exposed to the ton, may not forever tarry." He laughed. "It rhymes, do you see? Marry...tarry."

"I bid you good day, sir." The marquis picked up his hat and crop and strode toward the door.

"Wait," the duke cried. "There's a note. She left a note for you."

Desmond turned sharply, eagerly.

"Lord, sir, why didn't you say so? Where is it?"

The duke fumbled in the desk drawer. "Let's see now. Where did your mother put it? Ah, here it is."

My dear Lord Desmond,
Family concerns make it imperative that I return immediately to Scarborough. I trust you will forgive the hasty departure. Thank you for your many kindnesses.

Respectfully,
Samantha Scarborough

So cold and formal. "Family concerns?" he said aloud. "What concerns?"

"Rumour has it that Lord Scarborough is deep in dun territory."

The marquis stuffed the note in his pocket and strode again toward the door.

"Son," his father called. "Our business!"

"Later, sir, if you will. I must be off."

"Where to?"

"Scarborough!"

CHAPTER TWENTY

"THAT WAS QUITE A RUN, Miss Samantha," Tab said as he vigorously rubbed down Black Knight.

"Wasn't it, though? I think that was the best time ever!" In her old riding habit and scuffed boots, Samantha was busily rubbing the other side. She and Tab took turns, giving Black Knight his daily exercise and faithfully followed Hawkins's instruction for his care and feeding.

"He is sure to win the Classic."

"You and me, boy," Tab said. "Ain't none of 'em outrun us yet."

That was certainly true, Samantha thought. So why did Uncle Stanley look so worried? At first he had been jubilant, especially after a note from Lady Atterley accusing him of being a basket scrambler, pretending to be so wealthy when he was just taking advantage of poor little Matilda, trying to get hold of her fortune.

"Gad!" Lord Stanley exclaimed. "Didn't even know she had a fortune."

"She hasn't," Samantha declared. "For Lady Marlowe told me the Lindseys are as poor as church mice. That's just another of Lady Atterley's roundaboutations."

"Well, ain't no roundaboutation about this note. Let's me clear off the hook. She says she's glad my creditors caught up with me before I got the knot tied, and though she ain't one to gloat over another's bad fortune, it would serve me right if I should rot in prison." He chuckled. "Well, they say there's some good come out of everything."

"That's true." London and Somerset had been fun, even if it had all ended so dreadfully. And she would not think about that.

"Mind you, Sam, Tilly ain't so bad. But can you imagine Lady Atterley as a sister-in-law?"

Yes, Samantha thought, he had been happy then. He had gone off to Newmarket to post their entry and to place their bet. But since his return he had seemed a little downcast. Did he think Black Knight would not win?

"But we know you'll win, don't we?" She gave the horse an affectionate pat and Tab led him away to be fed.

As Samantha turned to leave the stable, the frisky little spaniel at her heels gave a series of ferocious barks. "Haro, do be quiet. What's to do?"

Her question was soon answered. It was Sir Malcolm Thomas. Haro never had liked him. Since their return to Scarborough, the squire had resumed his old habit of relentless pursuit. He called several times a week and was always bumping into her at the oddest moments. Like now. She forced herself to smile pleasantly. "Good morning, Sir Thomas. Out rather early, aren't you?"

"I caught sight of you galloping across the heath, and came to check on your progress. You've been giving him quite a workout, Samantha."

"Oh, no, it's the other way around. We just let him have his head."

"Readying him for Newmarket, eh?"

She nodded.

"No need to worry. Ain't another horse that can touch him. Everybody knows that. Pity."

Samantha looked up.

"A pity?"

"Odds against him are so low. I was going to place a bet, but it ain't hardly worth while."

"But, Sir Malcolm, he's sure to win. And by several lengths."

"That's just it, Samantha. You ain't listening. You see Black Knight's got such a reputation that it don't pay much to bet on him."

"Oh!" Samantha stared at Sir Thomas. That was it! That was what was bothering Uncle Stanley. Oh, she was such a goose! She had been to so many races and had never paid any attention to the betting. Even if Black Knight did win, there'd probably not be enough for Uncle Stanley's needs. How much did he need, anyway?

"What's the matter, Sam? You look as if you'd seen a ghost."

"Pray, Sir Malcolm, do excuse me. Uncle Stanley...that is, I have urgent business that I must attend. I must bid you good day." She left him abruptly and rushed to the house, Haro at her heels.

An hour later, she faced Mr. Simmons and Lord Scarborough over a table loaded with papers and a sheaf of bills. The sum due Uncle Stanley's creditors was staggering. The money that could possibly be won on Black Knight was a mere pittance.

"There, there, Sam," her uncle soothed. "I don't like you to be worried. Simmons here and Mrs. Kemper will look after you after I'm gone."

"Of course," Simmons agreed as he polished his glasses. "There's still the quarterly rents, and with Black Knight's stud fees, we'll soon be able to restock the stables."

"Oh, do be quiet," Samantha cried. Simmons actually looked relieved that Uncle Stanley would be away. "There must be some way. Let me think."

She felt the room closing in on her. Maybe in the open air... She reached for her cloak, but as she did so, they all heard the sound of a vehicle coming up the driveway.

She looked out to see the hired hack from the village. When the driver let down the steps and opened the door, a woman clad in a modest navy travelling dress emerged. Matilda Lindsey!

Lord Scarborough turned to Samantha in shocked surprise. "Good God, do you suppose they've turned her out? They wouldn't blame her because I turned out to be a bounder, would they?"

Though Samantha was as puzzled as he, she tried to reassure him.

A few moments later, when they greeted their visitor in the drawing room, Matilda turned an anxious, apologetic face to them. "Pray forgive me. I am sorry to intrude, but I wanted to speak with Lord Scarborough."

Uncle Stanley moved forward. "Of course, child. Is something troubling you?"

Samantha was surprised that he seemed more concerned than agitated.

"Yes," Matilda said. "There is something troubling me. That horrible note that Lenora sent you. And all the embarrassment we caused you."

Lord Scarborough rubbed his nose. "More embarrassment to you than to me."

"Oh, I was so mortified." She turned to Samantha. "You must know that I had no part in it. It was all Lenora's doing. Your uncle was so kind as to bring me a birthday present, and Lenora pretended it meant much more. Of course, I knew it didn't and she knew it. I told her I would make it clear to Lord Scarborough that he was under no obligation, but she whisked me off to the country so that I could not get in touch with him. Oh, I am excessively sorry. Please do forgive me."

"There is nothing to forgive," Samantha said as the poor girl paused for breath. "Please be seated and let me ring for some refreshment."

"No. Nothing, thank you. I shall soon be going."

"But you've come such a long way. How on earth did you get here?"

"I came by post. I'm on my way to Devon."

"The post?" Lord Scarborough exclaimed. "And what's in Devon?"

"That's my destination," Matilda explained. "And when I found I was to change at your village and was so near Scarborough, I hired a hack and came to bring you this." She held out the little box containing the turquoise ring.

Uncle Stanley held up his hand. "No, no. That's yours. I meant it for you."

"I know you did and I love it. It's the most beautiful gift I've ever received. And you are indeed the kindest man I have ever known." She turned such adoring eyes to Uncle Stanley that Samantha had to look away. "But this ring is very expensive, and I am persuaded that...forgive me, sir. I know you must need it more than I. Take it back or pawn it or whatever you do to offset your obligations."

Lord Scarborough gave a low chuckle. "I am afraid it would take more than that to offset my obligations." He took her hand and folded it over the little box. "No, you keep it. Wear it in remembrance."

"Oh, no, I couldn't. Not when you would be locked up in that—that place!" Matilda's eyes were filling with tears. "I know it will not offset all your obligations, but it will be a start. And I mean to send you something every month."

"You will not!" he exclaimed.

"Oh, please. Let me make up for the shabby way you were treated. I have a position now, you know. And I plan to send you every penny I earn until your debts are paid."

Lord Scarborough stared at her. "Never would I let you do such a thing!"

"Please don't say that. You have done so much for me. You were the one who told me not to be pushed but to do what I wanted to do. I wanted to be independent, so I contacted my old school mistress, who secured a position for me as governess for Lord and Lady Simpson at Levenshire. They have three children and—"

"I will not permit it," Lord Scarborough said quite loudly.

"Oh, please," she insisted. "I want to. I will send you every penny."

His eyes softened. "You'd do that for me?"

"I'd do anything for you," she said. Then, blushing under his direct gaze, she stammered, "Friends. You said we were friends."

"But I will not allow my fiancée to take a position as a governess."

Matilda blinked. "What did you say?"

Lord Scarborough fumbled in his pocket for his snuff box. "Governesses, you know. They get pushed and pulled more than anybody."

"But, that other...you said your—your—" Matilda faltered and was silent.

"Fiancée. It ain't the thing to be a governess." He put the snuff box back in his pocket. "You could stay here with Sam. You'd be taken care of all right and tight, till I get back. Maybe we can get a special licence and marry before I go."

Samantha could not fathom who was more surprised, she or Matilda. Or perhaps Uncle Stanley.

"Oh, Lord Scarborough, you are so kind. And I know it was not your intention—"

"No chance to declare my intentions." Uncle Stanley would not look at Samantha. "Devilish pouncing woman, your sister."

Matilda shook her head. "I know you never meant— No, I cannot allow it. I know you pity me, but—"

"Pity? An independent straightforward girl like you? No. Admire. I admire you, Matilda—Tilly."

"Oh, you are kind, but . . ."

"I ain't kind, either." Lord Scarborough took the little box from her and removed the ring. There was a glow of tenderness in his eyes as he slipped it on her finger. "Turquoise, you know. Like your eyes."

Samantha went quietly out, shutting the door behind her. She must have the luggage brought in and the hack dismissed. And tell Mrs. Kemper to prepare a guest room.

Having performed these chores, she called to Haro and went out for a brisk walk. Perhaps the air would clear her head and she could think of some way to help Uncle Stanley. He must not go to prison!

ON THE DAY that Lord Desmond left London for Scarborough, Jiggs, his coachman, was laid up with a bad case of lumbago. Jiggs protested loudly at the marquis's determination to make the journey without him, but was hastily consigned to the devil.

"Since when," Desmond declared, "have I been unable to handle a team of horses? And there's Clinton to relieve me." And to Clinton he confided that they could make better time without Jiggs. "He's getting devilish cautious, that man."

Clinton nodded agreement and braced himself for the rapid pace at which they were sure to travel.

So it was that the marquis was driving his own chaise when they neared the end of their journey. He had been driving for some time past Scarborough land and they were about a mile from the house, when he noticed a lone figure trudging toward them. It walked aimlessly, pausing every now and then to kick at a clump of dirt. Not alone, for near it a small dog scrambled from one side of the road to the other.

Desmond's heart leapt. Samantha! It had to be Samantha! He slowed his pace, not wanting to startle.

Samantha also slowed, shading her eyes to focus on the approaching carriage.

Desmond drew up beside her and looked down, trying to swallow the lump in his throat. She wore an old black riding habit, rumpled and dusty, and its skirt dragged unnoticed in the dirt road. The face that looked up at him had a smudge on one cheek, and no riband restrained the copper curls which fell in disarray about her neck and shoulders. This was the hoyden he had first met on that same road. Tousled, freckled, bedraggled, bewitching...entrancing! He felt an almost uncontrollable impulse to lift her into his arms and whisk her away to...where? Gretna Greene! For the first time, he felt an empathy with Rutherford. He jumped lightly down from the carriage, removed his hat and extended his hand.

Samantha's heart leapt in turn as she recognized the marquis. But then, suddenly, the humiliating memory of their last meeting came flooding back, and the smile of welcome froze. Blood rushed to her cheeks, and she murmured a halting greeting and turned away.

His untouched hand still outstretched, Desmond called a sharp command to Clinton to meet him at the manor house, then followed Samantha. He spoke harshly as he reached her side. "I'm not accustomed to having bargains I make with ladies of quality broken. We had an agreement, madam. One season in London for your sister, in return for you—your services to me."

Samantha sputtered with anger.

"That arrangement is done with, my lord. No longer will I serve as a shield to cover—"

"Stop! Don't tempt me, Samantha. Hurl that dastardly accusation at me one more time and I shall be inclined to take my horsewhip to you!"

"Oh, my lord, you put me in such a quake!"

"Don't play the shrinking violet with me, my girl! I know you don't fear me. But you'd best guard your tongue! You must know that if I truly loved a woman, no power on earth could stop me from making her my wife."

"Dear me!" she exclaimed in exaggerated surprise. "Can this be the same man who once used every power on earth to prevent being leg shackled?"

Her haughtily lifted eyebrow presented such a contrast to her bedraggled appearance that he couldn't help chuckling. "Touché! But time—and experience—are excellent teachers. That same man has discovered that, under certain circumstances, such a prospect could be infinitely agreeable." He bent toward her, his voice soft with meaning. He saw a flush stain her cheeks and saw the wide blue eyes regarding him quizzically, as if to catch his meaning. He saw those eyes suddenly flash with anger before she turned to walk away. He caught up and matched his stride to hers. "It is also the same man with whom you made an agreement."

"You could hardly expect me to continue that farce after what happened. No bargain, sir, could survive that episode on the road to Gretna Greene!"

"I'm sorry, Sam. I was a fool to have so misjudged you." Reluctant to admit that he'd been mad with jealousy, he continued rather lamely, "But what did you expect? Seeing you in those circumstances with that man!" He paused. "But, Samantha, please, I did not come to argue. I'm here…" He wanted to say, "To ask you to marry me," but instead he finished haltingly, "To—to see your uncle."

He caught the anxious look in her face as she turned to him, almost pleading, all thought of their quarrel vanished. "I beg you will not press him now," she said.

"Press him?"

"If he is under obligation to you."

"Obligation? Good God, Samantha, do you think every time I come, I come to collect a bet?"

"Oh. I'm sorry." Her voice was contrite. "You see, he spoke of some debt of honour, and I thought . . ."

"Gave his note, did he?"

"Yes. I thought— Forgive me, I thought it was you."

And I should have recognized that somebody's-in-trouble look on your face, he thought. *Arthur and now your uncle. Drat his infernal debts!*

Involuntarily his hand touched the pocket containing the diamond tiara. Probably worth close to the amount due Stanley's creditors. To present it now would be as out of place as it would look in that unkempt mass of tangled curls. He sighed. "Deep in the suds, is he?" Desmond should have remembered his father's remark about dun territory.

Samantha hesitated. "Well, I . . . that is . . ."

"Oh, girl, don't boggle at plain speaking now. I overheard your conversation in the library, remember?"

"I remember." She looked frankly up at him. "And it was kind of you—that plan that allowed us to visit your parents. Only, the thing is, I'm afraid we should not have gone to London at all."

"Didn't you enjoy your stay?"

"Oh, of course I did." She flushed. "That is, part—most of it." She lowered her head. "But it was so hard on poor Uncle Stanley. All those clothes . . ."

"Nonsense. It's not your clothes but your uncle's gambling errors that have landed him in the suds. Well, what's to do?" he muttered, almost to himself. What he would like to do was to pay off all those blasted debts. But he must tread carefully. That Scarborough pride. He must not again misread Samantha's character. If there was a way he could pay them without their knowing . . .

"I have been thinking and thinking," she said. "What do you suppose Black Knight would bring at the Tattersall auction?"

"Sell Black Knight?" he exploded. But even as he said it, he was thinking, that was one way. He could buy her blessed stallion for whatever they needed and give it back to her as a present—a wedding present.

"He's entered in the Newmarket Classic, you know, and I'm sure he'll win." She shook her head. "But not enough."

"Of course not. The plaque is worth only—"

"Oh, but we bet on him. I, that is, we raised a big stake and put it all on him, and I was sure we would make a lot of money." She sighed. "It seems he's too famous."

"Very low odds, I gather."

"Very low."

It came to him then, an idea he had been toying with a long time. "We'll just have to raise the odds," he said.

"Raise the odds? How do you do that?"

"Trust me."

CHAPTER TWENTY-ONE

DESMOND'S PRESENCE was like a balm to the whole household. Emily proudly displayed her new pearl earrings—an engagement present, you know—and talked with an almost matronly air of how she would soon be deserting Scarborough for Pendleton. Lady Travis had said it was a very good thing, because she would be a calming influence on Arthur. Poor dear Lady Travis. She had been so afraid Arthur would be captured by one of those flighty types.

Then she added as an afterthought, "Oh, and Matilda's come to marry Uncle Stanley. And that's a good thing, too, for she is very clever, you know."

Desmond managed to conceal his surprise as Lord Scarborough moved forward in the most natural way to present his betrothed. But he disclosed his puzzlement later to Samantha. "Gad, did that manoeuvring sister get him, after all?"

"No," Samantha answered. "It wasn't the sister."

He looked across the room at Lord Scarborough and remarked that "Yes, sooner or later we all get caught, if not by manoeuvre, then by love." He looked at her so intently when he said this that Samantha could not meet his eyes, nor prevent the surge of feeling this man always engendered in her. An eager and tantalizing expectancy, an aching yearning that held a promise of passion and pleasure that she only partially understood. She would not call it love! She shut her eyes, dismissing the memory of that kiss at Somerset. She forced herself to conjure up the vision of a beautiful dark-haired lady in white.

Oh, why had he come! She had been so busy since she left London, worrying about Uncle Stanley and trying to ready Black Knight, that she had been able to ignore her feelings. She would not call this fruitless longing love. For a moment she was angry that he had come. Then she remembered his words: "Trust me." He had come to help. He was kind. But kindness was not love.

She did, however, believe that it was love that had captured Uncle Stanley, for he seemed in much better spirits. She could not decide whether it was Matilda's or Desmond's presence that had revived him. Whatever it was, Lord Scarborough was almost like his old self, laughing frequently and talking as if he had not a care in the world.

It was, Samantha decided, Desmond's air of calm self-assurance. He exuded good humour and confidence, and the mood was catching.

Samantha, too, had caught it. When she came down to dinner she was radiant in a gown of bronze-green gauze, one of the London purchases. Tiny rosettes in a paler hue encircled her waist and were caught in a bunch at her hair, à la Monsieur Maurice.

Desmond abruptly left Emily in midsentence and moved toward her, his eyes bright with approval. He reached out and carefully rearranged one of the copper curls that Jenny had brushed in such haste.

"That's better," he said, then shook his head. "You are such a changeling, you know. A very good thing that you have those marks of distinction."

"Marks of distinction?" She could not take her eyes from his face.

"Freckles, my love. Like that dimple, they will always give you away."

Samantha felt a flush steal into her cheeks and she was glad that Lord Scarborough caught Desmond's arm and pulled him toward the fireplace. She joined Matilda on the sofa and tried to sort out her feelings.

My love. He had said *my love*! She must not be a goose, must not presume too much upon careless teasing words, upon friendship. For he was a friend, a very good one. Hadn't he always been there when she needed him? Even now, did she not suddenly feel that everything was going to be all right? She heard her uncle's booming voice and looked toward the fireplace.

"Why, of course it sounds like good news, my boy. But why all the secrecy? What is this crazy scheme that's going to make us all rich?"

"Can't tell you until I pull it off." Desmond reached a hand toward the snuff box Stanley had pulled from his pocket.

"May not work, eh?" Lord Scarborough's eyes were wary as he released the snuff box.

"To own the truth, it may not." Desmond took a pinch of snuff and held it to one nostril. Then he looked thoughtfully at Lord Scarborough. "It's a risk, man. And that's why I've picked you. Needless to say, I need a horse that's a sure winner, but I also need a man willing to take a chance. And who fits that category better than Stanley Scarborough!" He returned the snuff box as if it were a stamp of approval.

Stanley beamed, but raised questioning eyes to Desmond. "Damme it, man, what is the scheme? Let me in on it."

Desmond shook his head. "You'll just have to trust me. All right. All right. I admit, I'm using you to my own advantage. But what do you care if you stand to win a few guineas yourself! You do have a stake on your own horse, don't you?"

"Samantha's horse," Lord Scarborough corrected. "Yes, I have a stake, of course."

"Good," Desmond said, and looked toward Samantha. "Do you trust me, Sam?"

"Yes," she answered.

"Good girl." He went to her, taking both her hands in his. "Just make me one promise."

Samantha nodded. At the moment she would have promised him anything.

"Promise you will not start for Newmarket until I return."

She agreed, and indeed, that seemed an easy promise to keep, for the race was two weeks away.

He left after dinner, saying he must hasten if the scheme was to work. It was only after he had gone that Samantha allowed herself to ask the question, why had he come? She knew it was not as he had made Uncle Stanley think, that he had come seeking help in some scheme of his own. She knew his plans had been made that very day he walked with her and talked of raising the odds against Black Knight. What had he in mind?

Still, the other question haunted her more. Why had he come? To see her? No, she told herself, that was just wishful thinking. *My love.* She thought of a raven-haired beauty with flawless skin, and again told herself not to be a goose.

She had much to think of besides Desmond. So much depended on Black Knight. "Keep up the training," Desmond had said. He had gone to the stable, measured the horse very carefully, marking the figures on a pad. Could it be something about changing the weights? No, that was dishonest, and she knew that Desmond would never do anything dishonest. What could it be? "Trust me," he had said. She did trust him.

It was Hawkins who rebelled. When one week had passed and Desmond had not reappeared, the trainer appealed to Samantha. "Begging your pardon, ma'am, but we can't wait no longer. It'll take five days to walk him there, and he needs two days, best three, to rest up for the race. We need to start now."

"We'll wait," she said.

His gnarled hands gave Black Knight's bridle an exasperated twist. "Sure, he's a strong horse, Miss Samantha. But like your pa said, you don't push a horse too hard. Ain't no way he can win if he don't get a chance to rest before he runs."

Mention of her father brought a lump to Samantha's throat. He would have been disappointed to see Black Knight lose, as disappointed as he would have been if he could see the empty stalls in his stable. But her voice as she answered Hawkins was calm. "Lord Desmond will be here soon. Don't worry, Hawkins."

When two more days passed with no word from Desmond, Lord Scarborough began to look worried. "It's play or pay, Sam. If we don't show, we'll lose everything."

"We promised," she reminded him.

"I know." Uncle Stanley gave a helpless shrug and turned away.

It was Emily who spotted Desmond first. "Samantha, look," she called from her upstairs window. "It's a house on wheels."

Running to join her, Samantha was astounded. It was indeed a house on wheels. A small one, perhaps, but still a house on wheels, drawn by a team of six sturdy horses.

Seeing that this strange vehicle was preceded by Desmond's traveling coach, Samantha ran quickly downstairs and out the door.

"No, it's not a house. It's a horse carriage," Desmond explained to the family and various members of the household and stable who had gathered to see the strange contraption. "Rather crude, for we had to do the thing in a hurry. Kelsey, show them how it works," he called to the grinning man seated beside the driver of the vehicle.

Kelsey, a short stocky man with a cherubic face and heavy eyebrows above alert grey eyes, jumped down proudly to display his handiwork. Today he wore, in honour of the occasion, a conservative black coat and breeches instead of the usual workman's smock, but his square work-worn hands were clear indications of his trade. He explained how the back of the carriage opened from the top, forming a ramp by means of which the horse could be led inside. "Plenty of room," he explained. "Not only for the horse, but his feed, water, blankets and other necessities. And there's an opening in the roof for ventilation."

"Damme it, Desmond!" Lord Scarborough walked around the carriage in admiration. "So that's your devilish scheme. By Jove, it's a good one. Beats me how you got the thing built so quickly."

Desmond laughed. "Kelsey's not only the best wheelwright in London, he's the fastest. We put our heads together, and once we got the plans straight it went like clockwork. Matter of fact, he and his men worked without letup."

Samantha looked at Desmond. He, too, must have spent many sleepless nights, and stopped only to change horses on the drive from London. His clothes were rumpled and his eyes, though bright with excitement, looked tired. She found herself longing again to brush back that unruly lock of hair that fell across his forehead. She turned abruptly and instructed Jenny to tell Cook there would be guests for dinner.

Hawkins bent to inspect the leather springs. If his precious Black Knight was to ride in a carriage there must not be too much jolting. He pronounced the springs satisfactory and suggested they plan to leave immediately.

"No hurry," said Desmond. "We don't want to get there too soon."

"Right!" Lord Scarborough said with a chuckle. "Element of surprise. By Jupiter. I'll lay a monkey those odds

will skyrocket when Black Knight ain't there two days before the race. Capital idea, Desmond. Capital!" He roared
with laughter, slapping his leg. "Horse carriage! If that
don't beat all! I'll lay another monkey their eyes will pop
when we unload him just before the race."

They all joined in his laughter, and Desmond declared
the vehicle would always be known as the Scarborough
Wagon, though Kelsey wanted it called the Kelsey Horsecart. Anyway, Kelsey meant to have it patented.

They left for Newmarket two days later. Hawkins, with
Kelsey beside him, insisted on driving the new contraption that held Black Knight. Samantha and Matilda travelled with Desmond and Uncle Stanley in Desmond's
travelling coach, which was driven by Clinton, with Tab
beside him.

Mr. Kelsey told Hawkins that he was not about to miss
the first impression of his new horse carriage on the racing gentry. Likely to get orders for more conveyances of
the same type, he confided, for it was most definitely going
to be the coming thing.

There was only one overnight stop at a wayside inn, but
several stops to change horses and to exercise Black
Knight. The night before the race, they arrived at a small
inn on the outskirts of Newmarket. The maids, ousters and
the very few occupants gazed curiously at the strange vehicle, but since Desmond instructed Hawkins not to remove Black Knight until nightfall, no one knew what cargo
it carried.

"I'll ride into town to see how the betting goes," Desmond told Lord Scarborough. "It will not do for you to
show your face until the last minute. Your presence would
give the game away."

He returned ecstatic. His visit to the Jockey Club had
revealed that, in anticipation of his nonappearance, odds
against Black Knight had risen fifty to one.

NEXT MORNING Desmond himself went early to Newmarket, but cautioned that no one from Scarborough should arrive until shortly before the running of the Classic. Accordingly, Lord Scarborough escorted Matilda and Samantha to the stands a scant half hour before the race preceding the Classic. Their arrival was noted with surprise.

"Scarborough! Didn't think you'd show. Where's Black Knight, man? What happened?"

"Gone lame on you, eh? That's the way when you push 'em too hard!"

"And me with a hundred quid on him!" moaned a haggard-looking young man. "Curse my blasted luck!"

"Don't curse your luck till the race is run, my lad," advised Lord Scarborough.

The man turned an anxious, somewhat hopeful face toward him. "You mean he's going to show, after all?"

"Hawkins assured me he'd get him here in time for the race," Lord Scarborough answered as he calmly took a pinch of snuff.

"Devil a bit of it! In time!" shouted another. "You might as well have left him in the stable!"

Several angry men who had already bet on Black Knight crowded around Stanley, loudly protesting that they had been cheated. No horse who had just walked in could stay the course!

One bearded gentleman pointed a finger at Lord Scarborough. "I know what it is. Trying to run up the odds, eh? But you've waited too long I fear. Good Lord, man! This is the outside of enough!"

Matilda stirred uneasily on the uncomfortable bench and moved closer to Samantha. "It—it's different here," she whispered.

"Yes," Samantha agreed, taking her hand. "I know. It has not the fashion nor the comfort of Ascot." Nor of

Epsom, she thought as she glanced around and noted only two other women present besides themselves.

But this was the course with which Samantha was most familiar. Newmarket, noted for its training grounds and the Tattersall sales, drew the real horsemen, like her father, who loved and bred horses. There were other men, too, she thought, looking at the hardened avaricious faces around her—men who loved the power and prestige of owning the top of the lot. Here in Newmarket the races were harder, the stakes higher, the competition keener and more vicious.

"That man over there who keeps glancing this way," Matilda said. "He seems glad that Black Knight has not shown."

"Yes. He hopes he won't," Samantha answered. "That's Lord Bristol, who owns Sir Percy, the favourite after Black Knight." She also did not like the smirk on the face of the pudgy red-faced man, and was glad when the next race began and attention turned from the Scarboroughs.

She sat with her hands tightly clasped, almost oblivious to the thundering hooves and the shouts of the spectators. Like her father, Samantha had never gambled. But this one time there was so much at stake. She glanced at her uncle, who was shouting with the rest of the men. He seemed more calm than either she or Matilda. But, then, that lovable, carefree man was never concerned for himself. Now, however... Samantha shuddered at the consequences if Black Knight did not win. But he must. He would win. Samantha knew he was the best. She had looked over the entries and knew he could outdistance all of them, even Lord Bristol's Sir Percy, foaled out of Mad Molly by Bagdad. But she was worried about this new contrivance of Desmond's. They had all assured her that the horse would be comfortable, and that he would not be too jolted. But it was so new to him. Would it make him nervous and so affect his time? She was hardly conscious of the race or the discussions of the men around her.

Suddenly she heard a great shout, and turned with the others to see the arrival of the horsecart. Everyone was intensely interested in the strange new vehicle. Then there was a clamour and shouts of surprise as the princely black stallion was led down the ramp. Samantha's heart pounded. She longed to rush to him, place her face against the thick neck and murmur words of encouragement in his ear. She saw Tab, resplendent in the bright new green-and-gold outfit Matilda had fashioned from his old one. He mounted and led the horse around to the gate to be weighed in.

Samantha loved the races, but she had never been so tense in her life. Her stomach churned in apprehension and her mind raced with unsettling thoughts. Had they done everything right—neither over- nor undertrained the great horse? Oh, she mustn't be a ninny! Black Knight looked as sturdy and strong as ever. Tab? Was he over that slight cold he had the other day? He would certainly need to be alert, to use all his skill and cunning against these jockeys, some of whom were given to unfair and reprehensible tricks. The tension mounted, and she felt that she might burst with anxiety.

Then Desmond was beside her. She looked up into his cheerful confident smile, and was suddenly more eager and excited than anxious. Everything was going to be all right.

"I was waiting for Hawkins to arrive," he explained. "I saw the horses weighed in. We want no tricks, you know. Ah, here they are!"

Samantha stood on tiptoe to watch the horses pass in review. She glowed with pride at the sight of Black Knight. He was, of course, the finest. "Yet they are all such beautiful beasts," she said to Desmond. "It is a thrill to know one is looking at the finest horses in all of England."

A twinge of unease returned when the fourteen horses lined up for the start of the race. Black Knight was on the outside, while Sir Percy, his strongest contender had the most advantageous position, on the rail.

They were off! Matilda sank down on the bench, shut her eyes and assumed a praying position. But Samantha peered through her binoculars and watched, with Desmond and Stanley, every foot of the race.

Sir Percy took the lead immediately, while Black Knight lagged behind, boxed in by three other horses. He could not possibly break through, and it was with a sinking heart that Samantha watched him fall farther back. But then Tab seemed to lean forward, and with lightning speed, Black Knight bounded down the middle of the track and sped past the three horses. Sir Percy was still in the lead and, Black Knight, though gaining on him, was at the first turn, several lengths behind.

Samantha shut her eyes for a moment, linking her prayers with Matilda's. *Dear God, please.* The next moment her eyes opened to see that Tab had given the horse his head and in the stretch he was pulling ahead, gaining, passing all the others. At the second turn he was only two lengths behind Sir Percy. Samantha held her breath and her heart leapt as her horse sprinted forward. Now they were neck and neck. Then, as they made the last turn, Black Knight pulled ahead in a full gallop of such grace and beauty that Samantha's breath caught. Tab lay in a prone position, his face against the horse's neck. The beautiful black stallion, with steady rhythmic strides, crossed the finish line two lengths ahead.

"Oh, it was beautiful!" Samantha exclaimed, squeezing Desmond's hand before turning to throw her arms around her uncle. She moved aside as Matilda, with tears of joy and relief, took her place beside Lord Scarborough, and then they all went down to the winner's circle.

Mr. Kelsey stood a way apart, watching the crowd with interest. He was not to be disappointed in the spectacular effect of his new vehicle on the racing gentry. For years afterward, they talked of how only a few minutes before the race, Scarborough's horse, Black Knight, was unloaded from the Scarborough Wagon, to win the Classic Cup and a right princely sum that snatched Lord Scarborough from the very jaws of debtor's prison.

Of course, there had been a complaint from Lord Bristol, owner of the runner-up, Sir Percy, but the gentlemen of the Jockey Club found no rule requiring an entry to appear days or even hours before the race. The Scarborough Wagon, as it was already being called, was to change the course of racing history forever.

Mr. Kelsey stared at Lord Scarborough. Poor fellow, didn't hardly get to touch the purse he'd won. The Scarborough girl on his arm—the one in blue—had taken it from him and stuffed it in her reticule, muttering some gibberish about creditors and stocking a stable. She looked a shy little thing, but she acted like a real managing woman!

Not that Lord Scarborough seemed to mind. He just grinned good-naturedly at her and went on talking to all those folk around him who were congratulating him upon the ingenious idea. Lord Scarborough was receiving the name and the credit, neither of which he deserved.

Mr. Kelsey glanced at Lord Desmond, who did not seem to care a whit. He stood away from the crowd completely absorbed in that Scarborough miss, who was smiling up at him.

"You are quite remarkable, you know," Samantha said in her direct way. "So ingenious. Always getting people out of scrapes and making it look as if they had extricated themselves. Arthur, and now Uncle Stanley. You made him think he did you a favour."

"Oh, he did. I made a right tidy sum myself."

"Pooh! You know you did it only for him."

"No. For you." There was such a note of tenderness in his voice, such a caressing look in his eyes—and such a throbbing in her throat. Samantha felt a little dizzy and the noise about her sounded as if from a great distance.

"We can't talk here. Let me take you back to the inn." Desmond took her hand and led her through the crowd.

At the edge of the road they halted to let a coal cart lumber past. Samantha, suddenly alert, clutched his arm. "Oh, Mark, look."

He glanced about, but looked questioningly back at her.

"That horse. Didn't you see?" They were at his coach now, but Samantha hung back. "That coal horse. Did you notice those legs and the alert way he holds his head? He shouldn't be pulling a coal cart."

Desmond looked impatiently up at a grinning Clinton. "Go and buy that damned beast and arrange to have him brought here."

"Yes, sir." Clinton jumped down and ran toward the coal cart as Desmond handed Samantha into the carriage.

He looked a little exasperated, and she spoke softly, apologetically. "He really is good stock, sir. I don't think you will regret."

"I hope you won't. I had something else in mind."

"Something else?"

"For an engagement present."

"An engagement present?" Her pulse quickened. Did he really mean it?

"Samantha, darling, this farce has gone on long enough. Let's post our banns and be married as soon as possible."

He was looking at her with such yearning that she had a strong desire to fall into his waiting arms and feel his lips upon hers. But she could not banish the thought of a certain raven-haired beauty. She spoke hesitantly. "Are you sure that is your desire, my lord?"

"My desire! Oh, Samantha, don't you know how much I love you? When you were with Rutherford I was mad with jealousy. I said such terrible things. Can you forgive me, my sweet?" He took her hand in his and looked at her in his caressing way. "How could I accuse you of using such wiles? You are so frank and open. You have not a seductive feminine wile in your whole body!"

"Oh, I devoutly hope you are wrong, sir," Samantha said demurely, "for I shall certainly need them if I'm to compete with angels."

"Angels?" He seemed genuinely puzzled.

"Well, she surely had the look of one. For she was exquisitely beautiful, that lady I saw driving the high-perched phaeton. And I am sure that one of the matched bays was my beloved Bonnie." She had tried to speak lightly, but her voice broke and she could not look at him as she added, "I was persuaded that she must have meant a great deal to a man who had the pick of the Scarborough Stables and chose Bonnie for her."

"But it was for you. For love of you that I chose Bonnie!"

"For me?"

"Clinton told me I should have chosen Black Knight. But even then I could see how much you loved the beast, and I would not have taken him for the world."

"Oh. Oh, yes," she said slowly, remembering that Uncle Stanley had given her the horse the next morning, saying that Desmond had suggested it. She had thought it kind of him. But kindness, she reminded herself, was not love.

"Oh, Sam, stop looking at me in that doubtful way! Sweetheart, we must talk. And I can't explain anything to you when you sit away from me, looking so prim and proper." Deliberately he reached over, and, taking the pins from her hat, removed and tossed it aside. "Come here." She did not resist as he pulled her toward him. With his arms around her, he began gently to remove her gloves. He spoke softly against her hair. "Do you remember, when we first met, how you said I had a right to my reputation?"

She nodded against his chest.

"Well, that reputation, that past, ended almost from the very first moment I met you. The phaeton, my love, was a farewell gift—both to Angel and to the life I had before you came into it." She looked up, wanting to believe him. He did not take his eyes from hers as he lifted her hand and held it against his cheek. "Since you captured my heart there has been room for no other woman. Nor will there ever be."

"But that night, when I came to your room." The memory aroused something primitive in her and she wanted to scratch at that slight stubble of beard in a jealous rage. "I know she was there," she said, trying to pull her hand away.

"Her visit that night was as much a surprise to me as was yours. She came in anger. Because she had not seen me in weeks and had received no answer to her many notes and—" He had spoken rapidly, but now he broke off. She saw the discomfort in his face and she knew he wanted her to know what he was too much a gentleman to say. Never would he tell her how hard it was to rid oneself of an ambitious mistress to whom one had been particularly generous. Sometimes a rake, but always a gentleman, she thought tenderly as she allowed her hand to caress that stubble of beard.

"Oh, Samantha, I love you so much." His lips were against her sensitive palm and she felt a tremor, warm and sweet and savage, stir through her whole being. "It was that night that I made Angel understand that our relationship was completely and irrevocably severed. And," he added, his brow creasing into a frown, "if you had not gone so completely cold on me, I would have made it known to you, as I did to her, that I was passionately in love with you. And only you."

"Cold? Oh, yes, that was what I was trying to be. For it was I who was mad with jealousy. I couldn't bear the thought of your loving another woman," she gasped as she reached up to do what she had so longed to do. She tenderly brushed back that stray lock of hair and timidly traced a finger across his lips. "Mark, I was so ashamed. But I couldn't bear it. Every time I thought of you with her I wished to scream and kick and scratch at you!"

"What a wildcat you are!" he said with a laugh, clasping her in such a passionate embrace that she could hardly breathe. "You have my full permission to do just that in the unlikely event I should give you cause." His lips travelled across her face, then fastened upon hers with such sweet possession that her emotions swirled and skidded and her body throbbed with an urgent longing she only vaguely understood. She returned his kiss with reckless abandon, her hands frantically fondling his neck and shoulders and running through his thick hair.

She heard him groan, felt his arms close fiercely about her as he murmured softly against her ear, "Oh, my darling Samantha. Don't you know that no woman could move me as you do?" His voice became a whisper and he punctuated each word with a kiss on her ear lobe, her neck, her cheek. She nestled closer, revelling in each kiss, full of such passion and such tender promise, sending a fire surging through her veins, that she hardly heard his words, "I love you so! My sweet wild hoyden!"

Harlequin Romance

Harlequin Regency Romance™

COMING NEXT MONTH

#3 THE TART SHOPPE by Phyllis Taylor Pianka
When Lady Constance Seaforth becomes ill from an
earlier eaten pigeon pie, she chooses the closest and
most convenient inn to recover her health. She has no
knowledge that the ''inn'' is a busy brothel or that the
gentleman who visits her in the middle of the night is as
mixed-up as she is. When they meet again in London,
Lady Constance is determined to even the score with
the infamous Earl of Marshfield.

#4 MIDSUMMER MASQUE by Coral Hoyle
On the night Julia Witton attempts to escape an
arranged marriage, all she gains are a black eye and a
leather pouch thrown from a passing carriage. She
discovers the pouch contains secret documents about
the war in France and hides them. She is suspicious
when a foppish botanist turns up at her home near
Bath to study the flora and fauna, especially when she
realizes that he considers her the most interesting
specimen worthy of scrutiny!

ANNOUNCING . . .

The Lost Moon Flower
by Bethany Campbell

Look for it this August
wherever Harlequins are sold

HR 3000-1